THE ROBBERY AT THREE WELLS

Fred N. Kimmel

Six brawny cowboys assailed Will Seven
when he drifted into the sleepy town of
Three Wells and smiled at the banker's
daughter. Outraged, the wiry Will rose
from the dust and whipped them single-
handed. His battle is witnessed by a fat,
good-natured blackguard named
Delevan who, after dealing him a
paralyzing blow to the breastbone to
teach him manners, offers Will a job in
his specialty . . . bank robbery.
Gargantuan portions of wildness follow
as our hapless young hero finds himself
fighting on both sides of the law, with
his loyalties planted firmly – somewhere
in between.

THE ROBBERY AT THREE WELLS

Fred N. Kimmel

Curley Publishing, Inc.
South Yarmouth, Ma.

Library of Congress Cataloging-in-Publication Data

Kimmel, Fred.
  The robbery at three wells / Fred N. Kimmel.—Large print ed.
    p. cm.
  1. Large type books. I. Title.
  [PS3561.I422R6   1991]
  813'.54—dc20
  ISBN 0-7927-0841-5 (lg. print)   90-15487
  ISBN 0-7927-0842-3 (pbk: lg. print)   CIP

Published in Large Print by arrangement with Donald MacCampbell, Inc. in the United States, Canada, the U.K. and British Commonwealth and the rest of the world market.

Distributed in Great Britain, Ireland and the Commonwealth by CHIVERS LIBRARY SERVICES LIMITED, Bath BA1 3HB, England.

Printed in Great Britain

To Fred, the straightest of the outlaws, and to Dr. Kepes who really set things straight.

1.
The Bum

There was a big smear of blood on his face and one eye was swollen shut. Yet he grinned up at them, white teeth spotted with the blood oozing from his torn lips. A swatch of his hair covered most of the pale gray eyes.

There were six of them – tough cowboys, all in the pay of Dan Elgin. As he slowly pushed himself up from the dust, the six cowboys gathered around him once more; they had all started for their horses believing the bum to have had enough. A big black-bearded cowboy caught him under the jaw with the point of his boot, sending him back onto the seat of his pants. A chorus of laughs greeted the blow. The bum shook his head, felt his jaw, and he smiled a bloody smile.

The cowboy with the black beard spoke.

"Stay down, bum; stay down on the ground where you belong."

"Aw, let him get up," entreated one of the others; "he's game for more of the same."

The rest of the men voiced approval, for

1

they were enjoying the fight – the odds being what they were.

"I'd like to get up," said the bum, "but you fellows sure do crowd in close in a fight. What's the matter – you afraid that if I get up I might lick a couple of you, eh?"

Growls came from the throats of the six indicating disbelief, yet more than one of them had a battle scar from this fray.

The big cowboy with the black beard scowled down. He said: "Listen, tramp, we ain't lettin' you up, see; you gotta crawl if you wanta get out of this. Look what you did to Bob here: he can hardly see; and Harry's arm is hurt – it's hangin' limp, like; he ain't gonna be able to throw a rope for some time. It beats me how a rawhide like you can sneak a mule's kick into that fist of yours. I've run into two of your haymakers, and while I can't believe it I sure can feel it. You don't get up today, tramp! You think you're pretty tough, and maybe there *is* a little magic in the dukes, but down there on the ground we can start stompin' you to death any time you're ready – so stay down and live!"

The stranger scowled at them.

The leader of the group walked to the bedraggled mare that the bum had ridden into town, undid the bridle from the hitch rack, and added: "So's you get the message,

2

we'll take your hoss; that oughta make some impression that we mean business, and you won't forget the day you make a pass at Dan Elgin's daughter." He started to lead the horse toward his own mount, which stood nearby, tethered to the hitch rack.

The bum started up, a cry on his lips. It was obvious that the other meant in all earnestness to take his horse.

The pointed boot of another of the six lashed out, but somehow that cowboy had become strangely uprooted and was hurtling through the air. He crashed down among two of his fellows, the force of his landing carrying them to earth with him.

A startled cry leaped from the throats of the two remaining attackers at having been so startlingly exposed to the risk of two against one. They dashed at the tigerish stranger, but with a snarl he side-stepped them, grasped the wrist of the closer, and spun him so that he cracked skulls with his astounded partner. The two cowboys were now at rest in the dust, one gazing glassy-eyed at the noonday sun and the other rubbing his head and mumbling, his ferocious temper of a moment before strangely dissipated.

Delevan shifted his ponderous, obese form in his chair on the veranda of the hotel, watching the fray closely. The heat of the day,

3

the fierceness of the struggle before him, and his own great weight forced the sweat from his body in great droplets that stood out on his brow, face, and neck, and he dabbed at them with a large multicoloured handkerchief. He wore no chaps nor did he carry a Colt on his hip, but it was known that he wore a shoulder holster encasing a tailor-made weapon. His bushy, Machiavellian eyebrows dipped down in the center, and his face was heavily jowled much like that of a bulldog. When he raised his hat and passed a handkerchief over his head it could be seen that, except for the hair along the sides and around the back of his head, he was completely bald. His nose was straight and long, and might have been called classic had it presided over a face other than his. His small eyes darted about, following the lightning movements of the combatants.

Delevan had been sitting on the long porch of the hotel when the bum had ridden into town. He had seen him dismount and fuss with the nag he rode. He had watched him go through his pockets, come up with a piece of change, go into the saloon, and come forth with a bottle of warm beer.

Delevan had also been watching when Dan Elgin drove his buggy into town with his pretty daughter Mary as a passenger. From under the shade of his hat brim he had seen

4

the bum finish his bottle of beer and walk to the buggy of the banker to inspect it. He had also noticed the bold appraisal that the disheveled yet good-looking stranger had made of the girl who was waiting in the buggy for her father. Delevan had smiled when the bum had spoken to Mary.

Amused at the attempt of the wiry newcomer to make conversation, Delevan had also noted the approach of the girl's father, the look he cast at the intruder, and his subsequent order to Chuck Mace, the strong-arm foreman of the Elgin Ranch.

He had seen the first part of the battle when the fire of youth and pride had carried the tramp to temporary success against overwhelming odds, but this he had dismissed with a grunt and forced himself to look the other way, for he knew the stranger would succumb to the weight of numbers before long. He hadn't observed Chuck Mace kick the bum in the face nor had he seen him start to take his horse, but Delevan stared astounded as the man left the three entangled cowboys he had bowled over a moment before and turned to Chuck Mace.

The foreman had scarcely turned to face his assailant when the tramp was upon him with savage, skillfully cutting blows. Mace, a brawling type of fighter, covered his face and

5

sank to one knee beneath the precision and scientific fury of the youth's punches.

It was over as quickly as that. The result of the fight caused great excitement among the spectators, but probably no heart beat so wildly as did that of Delevan. The fat man spoke softly to his companion on the porch.

2.
Delevan

The gaunt countenance of Cy Storker scowled back at Delevan. It was clear that he wanted no part of the fighting tramp, but the look of his chief was all he needed to start him up from his chair. He turned to the other and said:

"Well, where do you want him? He looks like a big drink of trouble to me. Sure you know what you're doin', eh?"

"Bring him to the room," commanded Delevan, and with that short directive he arose and went through the door of the hotel.

Storker stepped from the porch and walked with a slight limp toward the bum. At the sound of the step the stranger turned and glared at him.

"What do *you* want?" he asked.

"Just a little information, son," said Storker with a grin that showed his uneven teeth.

"About what?" asked the tramp, turning his back on the thin man as though there was nothing to fear from him. Although it was perceptible to no one, his shoulders tensed, for he suddenly found himself fearing the gaunt man more than any of the rough cowboys he had just upended. He had turned his back because he didn't want to hold the stare of the deep-set, black eyes of the other.

"About what you're goin' to do for the next ten minutes," answered Storker, deftly rolling a cigarette.

The other turned and gazed hungrily at the tobacco and papers. Storker offered nothing but a grin.

"Ten minutes from now," said the tramp, "I'm putting miles between me and these boys with headaches." He motioned to the cowboys who were dusting themselves off and scowling at him.

"There's a fellow that would give an awful lot to talk to you for ten minutes," said Storker.

"The sheriff, eh?" said the stranger with a scowl. "You're his deputy, hunh?"

7

"Nope." The gaunt man laughed, dragging on his cigarette. "You're runnin' from these boys, eh?"

The other scowled, his jaw muscles tightening. "I'm not runnin' – just leavin'."

"This gent that wants to see you," began Storker, "don't like these fellows himself. You talk to him for ten minutes, an' he'll see that you get out of town in one piece."

"Okay," said the bum, growing curious. "This is such an unfriendly place, I might just go talk to this friend of yours. Never see such a town as this – just step up and smile at a girl, and *blam!* Six guys start hitting you."

"Follow me," said Storker as he limped off across the street.

They went to the hotel and upstairs to the room of Delevan were Cy Storker pushed open the door. The huge man stood in the middle of the room, his coat off and his white shirt and shoulder holster revealed. The tramp stared in without entering. He stepped back and looked through the crack where the door hinged to make sure no one was hiding there. Satisfied that all the danger there was, was in the open, he stepped into the room. His flesh prickled as some strange, electric impulse warned him of the power around him.

8

He grinned. "Hello, fatty," he said, for it was always his way to start things off right for himself, whatever the situation.

"Hello, son," said the fat man, his brows arching slightly.

"You want to see me about somethin'? What is it?"

"When's the last time you had a good meal?" asked Delevan.

"Twenty-three years ago."

"Smart, ain't he? I'd like to take a little of that smartness off him," hissed Storker, a knife appearing in his hand.

"Put down that toad stabber, skinny," the tramp said derisively; "you might cut yourself."

"Cy here is pretty handy with a knife, son," cautioned Delevan.

"He still might cut himself."

"Put it up, Cy," commanded the chief.

The knife disappeared, and Storker turned with a frown and sat down on the bed.

"How'd you like a job?" asked Delevan.

"I don't work, I just travel," said the bum.

"Yeah, I can see your hands are kind of soft looking," murmured Delevan, "but how'd you like a job traveling?"

"A job traveling?"

"Well, yes, sort of. We move around a bit – eh, Cy?" said the fat man with a knowing

9

wink at the other.

"I'll bet you do move, fatty. In fact, you're probably two jumps ahead of about six sheriffs right now, eh?"

"Nobody takes my trail," said Delevan, matter-of-factly.

"What's the job, today? You want me to do your killing or something like that, eh? Well, let Croaker here, or whatever his name is, do it for you! I don't kill and I don't work for rats like you."

Delevan listened to the comments of the stranger, appearing not in the least perturbed by the implications of anything the other had said. He smiled gently and dabbed at the perspiration on his upper lip. He stepped between the newcomer and the door; his step was surprisingly light and graceful, a characteristic of most heavy-set people.

"You do talk tough, kid!" the fat man said with a smile.

"Well, I *am* tough," admitted the bum.

"Bah, a street fight!" scoffed the fat man. "What is that – a few fools lose their heads and throw a lot of wild punches – what does that prove? Any cool head can pick his way through a blind bunch like that. Why, I could lick ten wild punchers like those you were against. One straight one to the chin while they're all hollerin' and swingin'

10

with their eyes closed. That's no test of toughness." He ended with a contemptuous look at the stranger.

The tramp said: "You – you talk about bein' tough! Step aside, or I'll belt you one! How much'll you give me if I do that?"

"I'll give you a dollar." The stout man smiled. "Fifty cents' worth of experience and fifty cents' worth of pain."

"By Gawd, I'll collect it, too!" As the stranger jumped back, preparing to strike, his eyes gave away the point of attack, for while he had talked of hitting the other in the face, his eyes had been continually wandering toward the immense belly before him. He leaped forward, swinging a vicious uppercut at the soft-appearing paunch of the huge man.

So quick was the motion of the tramp, so viciously low his blow, Cy Storker leaped from the bed with a cry of pain of his own – anticipating the agony that was soon to be his chief's.

The bum struck deep into the abdomen of the heavy man. A smile twisted his face as his fist disappeared in the immensity of fat; but just as quickly as he had struck, his fist suddenly encountered stringy, vibrant muscle that seemed to gather strength and force and actually hurl his hand backward. The bum gasped in disbelief.

The huge balled fist that traveled toward him struck him a terrible, numbing blow flush on the breastbone. For the second time that day the bum was on the seat of his pants. The blow had temporarily paralyzed him; he fought for air. His face turned red, then purple, and just as it seemed that he would smother, a small quantity of air came to his bursting, burning lungs. The next came easier; slowly, painfully, he began to breathe again. He looked at the fat man with new respect.

Cy Storker was standing over him, laughing. When he perceived that the stranger could speak at last, he chortled: "How'd you like another half-dollar's worth of that, bum?"

"That was paid in full," said the tramp, trying to smile.

"How about that job, kid?" asked Delevan.

"Talk some," said the stranger. "I'll set here a while, and rest, and listen."

3.
Haste Makes Waste

"We'll eat a little; then we'll talk some," announced Delevan.

He glanced at Cy, who immediately left the room to return moments later with the anxious hotel clerk. Delevan, with the aplomb of the seasoned gourmet, ordered a meal for the three of them to be brought to the room.

It proved that Delevan was indeed a gourmet – even if the quality of the hotel's cooking was not worthy of his talent, for when the bum pushed back from the table he had eaten two whole roasted chickens, while the thin Cy had done for one of the birds, but the ponderous Delevan was cleaning the meat from the bones of his fourth. All of the trimmings were served as well, along with a delicious dry wine of which they drank several bottles.

The bum sat back, drew the flame of a match deeply into a fine Havana cigar and, glancing down at his ragged clothes, blew forth the smoke in a long, thin stream. He smiled. He had enjoyed the meal. He wondered how he must pay for it, for it was not his way to accept a gift without countering in some manner, even though the manner of payment might not always be appreciated by the other.

He said: "When you order food, Delevan, you order good; when you eat, you eat a lot; when you punch a gent in the chest, you go all the way and cave in his breastbone – what else do you do?"

"A little of everything, my brash young friend; but let me ask the questions, for I did buy the meal."

"Ask."

"What's your name?"

"Seven."

"Seven what?" asked the fat man, arching his brows.

"Seven nothin'. My name is William Seven."

"Will Seven!" exclaimed the fat man, turning to Cy, an amused expression on his face. "What do you think of that?"

Storker shrugged his shoulders. "It suits him. Seven is a lucky number."

"You think he's lucky, eh?" shouted Delevan, jumping up. "By heaven, that's the way he strikes me too! Lucky for us, eh, Storker?"

"Not lucky for us," frowned Storker,

looking jealously at the bum, "lucky for hisself, that's what he is. Just a good-for-nothin' lucky bum that thinks he's tough."

Delevan sank back into his chair with a slight belch, a slightly saddened expression on his expressive face. "But Cy, he's tough – you've seen that."

"Licked a bunch of cowboys is all," said Storker, looking at the floor as if the feat were nothing.

"Not that," said Delevan, looking at his confederate. "You saw the way he recovered from the punch."

"That's right," said Cy. "He ate, too. Wilson spent a month in the hospital after he took one of those. Maybe he *is* tough, I dunno."

"No, I think you're right, Storker," said the fat man, his eyes twinkling. "He's tough enough for us, but he don't have it here." He pointed to his stomach.

"What's that?" asked Seven. "You saying I ain't got guts?"

"That's a crude way of putting it," admitted the other.

"Well, you're nuts!" exclaimed Seven, glaring at the fat man.

"You're handy with your hands and you're tough for a little guy. What's your height? What's your weight?" asked Delevan.

15

"Five-eleven and a half and one hundred-eighty even," said the bum.

"Well, as I said, kid, you're scrappy as hell and you seem to have nerve – but can you use your head to go with it? The head is the thing: give me a midget with a brain any day to a dumb giant. I had an idea for a minute there – I thought of a thing you might be able to do – but it's ridiculous!" He stopped talking and started to laugh, nodding at Storker as though the other had been right all along in his lowly opinion of Will.

"What're you two guys laughin' at? What's this thing you want done? I'll bet I can do it – by God, I know I can! But if it's murder, get yourself another man. I don't do murder."

"It's not murder, son," answered Delevan; "but how would *you* do murder? You don't carry any gun, I see; nor do you look like the kind that would be hiding a knife."

"I sold my gun," Will admitted.

"To buy a better one, eh?" nodded the fat man, "a little sneak gat that not even Storker can see, hunh?"

"No, I sold it to buy food," said Seven, glaring at the fat man.

"How long since you ate – before today, I mean?"

"Two days."

"By Gawd, did you hear that Storker?

16

He's been two days without food!" exclaimed Delevan, exuberant. He added: "You don't murder, eh? What if it's kill or be killed?"

"I face that when I come to it." Will shrugged.

"Good, I don't like anyone working for me that feels any other way," said Delevan.

"What do you do?" asked Seven.

"Anything that brings high profit," said the other with a wink.

"What'll my cut be?" asked Will.

"A third of anything that comes." Delevan smiled.

"A third!" echoed Seven. It was a split that he was not used to in his limited business dealings.

"A third of the whole," said the fat man, "not just a third of the profit — there's a deal of difference, you know."

Will Seven nodded appreciatively. "What do I do for this third?"

"Nothin' much," said Delevan: "just ride five hundred miles north of here, get a piece of paper, ride back, and make love to a girl. That's all you have to do."

"That sounds easy enough — all except the last part. I ain't no gigolo. Who's the girl?"

The fat man smiled. "Same tasty dish you got kicked in the face for outside," he answered.

"Her? I wouldn't marry her for a third of California! She's too heavy – I like thin girls. Find a thin girl, an' I'll do it."

"Listen, you don't have to marry the girl or anything like that. Just spark her a little is all – till we've made certain – er – arrangements. You can find out a few things for us while you're doing it; we'll handle all the rest."

"On the level?" asked Seven, "I don't have to marry the girl, hunh?"

"Absolutely not," declared Delevan. "Marriage has nothing to do with it."

"My horse ain't the kind for a five-hundred-mile ride," said Will, facing up to the fact.

"You'll have the best of horses; you'll start out on one that will go like the wind and you'll come back on one that'll streak across the ground like greased lightning."

"Where do I pick up this scrap of paper?" asked Will, becoming more interested with the description of the horses he was to ride.

"A fellow has it on him." Delevan smiled. "Perhaps you've heard of him. His name is Costain."

The youth gasped. "Lee Costain!"

"Long Lee himself," admitted Delevan.

"Long Lee Costain the train robber!" Will whistled. "Why, he's the longest drink of poison in this state."

"Sure; only, he ain't in this state any

18

more. Besides that, he's washed up – on the run, and frightened out of his wits that any second someone will turn him in for the big reward."

"He's runnin' scared, eh?" asked Seven, but not believing the words.

"Yes, he's a has-been – he's drunk his nerves to the brink, and a child could make him jump with a toy gun. You won't have any trouble getting the paper from him. He's alone, without a friend to guard his back; he's getting gray-headed and he shakes like a leaf. He –"

"If he's that bad," interrupted Seven, "how come I need a horse for comin' back that streaks like lightning?"

Delevan cleared his throat. "The quicker to begin our work."

"How do I find this feeble old cuss, and why don't you sneak up and get the paper yourself? – if it's so easy," asked Seven.

"I couldn't sneak up on a wooden Indian," declared Delevan.

"That's true enough," said Seven, regarding the bulk of the other.

"And," continued Delevan, "I've got to stay here to see that everything stays tied down at this end."

"Okay, Delevan. What does this paper look like?"

"You can't miss it, kid – it's around his neck on a string!"

Seven winced.

Delevan eyed Will keenly. "Got you scared, eh?"

"Nope," said Seven. "It don't scare me much – not if it's as easy as you say. How do I find Costain?"

"You know the rods?" asked the fat man.

"Yeah, I've been on the rods some. Costain likes the railroads too, don't he? Only, he goes after 'em for a different reason than I ever did. I used to steal a ride once in a while, but he's used to takin' the whole train."

"That's right," and Delevan laughed at the comparison.

"How much is the bundle you talk about divvying three ways?"

"Six hundred thousand is the whole! You get $200,000 if you bring back the paper – we're that sure of the rest. You'll find Costain somewhere around Gaffert – have you ever been in Gaffert?"

"Once."

"Good. Costain is planning to hold up the train from Cleary – a money shipment – but he'll probably lose his nerve at the last minute! When do you want to start for Gaffert – perhaps after a couple of days' rest?"

"I'll start at dark," said Seven. "Get that

20

horse you was talkin' about, and I'll be back in two weeks."

"Two weeks, hell!" grunted the fat man. "We'll look for you in thirty days. And don't foul up $200,000. 'Haste makes waste,' you know."

4.
The Eavesdropper

The three men stood in the dark shadows behind the hotel regarding the gigantic jet-colored horse that stood saddled and ready before them. Cy Storker held the bridle of the great Barb and stroked his small soft muzzle.

Seven murmured: "He'll run like the wind; I've no doubt of that much," he said, walking around the animal. "But where do I get the horse that will bring me back? This one looks like he could go both ways."

"Costain has a horse called Bayard. If you get the paper you might as well take the horse, for he can't be beaten by Black Boy here. If Costain has his wits and that running devil of a Bayard, he'll be on your heels all the way back here."

Will grinned, and stepped into the saddle. Horse stealing, at least in this case, did not go against his nature. He looked down at the heavy-set crook and said: "Any other advice, O Great Fat Father?"

"Don't be funny," Delevan scowled. From under his arm he took a package and unwrapping it, brought forth a holstered Colt revolver and shell belt. He hung the gun belt over the horn of the saddle and said: "This gun is one of my old ones. You'll find it works well and shoots straight."

"I suppose," said Seven with a knowing nod.

"Have you got the other package, Cy?" asked Delevan of the other, who still held the bridle of the nervous horse.

"Here are the duds," whispered Storker in a hoarse voice. He handed over a package which Delevan fastened behind the saddle.

"As soon as you can, change into these clothes," ordered Delevan.

"What's wrong with the ones I've got on?" queried Will.

"You look like a bum – on a prince's horse," explained the fat man harshly. "You stand out too much. These clothes match the horse – not you; although I must say that you'll probably be quite handsome in them. At least, nobody you run across will think

22

you're a horse thief."

"Is that all, Delevan?" asked Seven, staring down.

"Here's $500 to grease your way," said Delevan pleasantly.

Cy Storker gasped.

"Thanks," said Seven, glancing at Storker. "This ought to last me till I get to Gaffert; then I'll wire you for more!"

As Cy Storker groaned, and before Delevan could do more than curse, Will booted the horse with a spur. The great black stallion lurched down in the hindquarters, then sprang away from them at a gallop, leaving only the sound of his hoofbeats and the trailing laughter of Will Seven in their ears. An iron-shod hoof struck a rock and left a brief spark somewhere in the distance; then not even the hoofbeats came back to their ears.

Cy gazed after the rider and mumbled, but Delevan patted his confederate on the back reassuringly, and together they turned and reentered the hotel.

Will pushed the big horse called Black Boy into a stretching gallop in a northerly direction before he pulled back at the reins and eased the gait. Well away from the town of Three Wells he stopped and listened. He was, he thought, beyond possible detection of Delevan and Storker, so he rode in a leisurely circle around the town and returned from the opposite direction. Because he thought it prudent to allow for a sufficient time to elapse, he took minutes to put the big black stallion through his paces.

He was familiar with the satin-smooth gallop, but he found that the horse could amble, and this was a surprise, for few riding horses are good at it, that is, high-spirited horses such as the one he now found himself having the good fortune to bestride. Next he tried the stallion at a trot, and even this most difficult of gaits for the rider he found to be exceedingly comfortable. At a lope he decided that the animal could maintain such a pace all day. Next he brought the horse to a walk, and so approached the back of the hotel once more.

As he stealthily dismounted and tethered the horse, he decided he would not abandon Black Boy for the flight back from Lee Costain. Will moved cautiously around the hotel building; he negotiated the narrow alley and inspected the street. Between the passing of a stumbling drunk and the approach of a buggy, he shinnied up one of the columns of the veranda and found himself crouching on the roof of the long, rambling structure.

From window to window he crept, making himself small as he passed each patch of light. At last he paused at the window of Delevan and Storker. The bottom half of the window was open, and the curtains fluttered out into the warm night air. He sat down to one side and, with his back resting against the thin wall, listened to the voices floating from within.

He heard the rich baritone of Delevan saying: "It's no risk I tell you. The kid'll be back before a month is up."

"He's walked off laughing at us, that's what he's done," argued Storker. "He's got Black Boy, your best horse, and a cool $500 cash, more money than he ever saw before. He's probably in the next town now, blowing it on a drunk; he'll wake up in the morning with all his money lifted and sell the horse. That piece of doing will cost you $2,000."

Will smiled. He could smell the sweet smoke of one of Delevan's Havana cigars coming from the window.

Delevan's voice purred reassuringly.

"You're wrong, of course. This Will Seven, he ain't like any ordinary tramp. Maybe he ain't worth a damn, and he's a no-good saddle bum and a dirty fighter, but that's all right because he ain't too big; besides, he's probably a petty crook and a lot of other things; but still, when he tells me he'll do somethin', I believe him."

25

"You're sure behavin' funny about this guy, Del," said Cy, "I never knew you to get mushy over a good-lookin' kid."

"It isn't that he's good-looking; he's got sand – grit and spunk. Listen, I can't get close to Costain and you'd be bumped off before you got out of the saddle, but somehow Will's goin' to get that paper off Lee's neck. I feel it in my bones; I'd bet all the money we got."

"Aw, I wouldn't bet ten cents on that tramp. Besides, you lied to him. What's he goin' to do when he finds out that Costain hasn't even hit his peak yet? What's he gonna do when he finds out Costain is surrounded with fifteen or twenty prime fightin' men?"

"He'll get by all of them," predicted Delevan.

"Yeah," began Cy, "maybe he will; but what's gonna happen when Lee Costain lays eyes on Black Boy? That's a horse *nobody* would forget, let alone Costain."

"Well, that's goin' to be a hard thing for Seven to explain, but I tell you, Cy, he's got more gall than Caesar – he'll bring it off somehow or other, mark my words."

"Even if he got close enough to Costain to snatch that paper while Lee was sleepin', he still has to give him the slip and get back here. Nobody ever gave Costain the slip. He can't brace Lee with a gun – nobody can. If he does

26

try to go through with it, he's a dead duck and you know it."

"I think not," declared Delevan.

Will froze as he heard the ponderous fat man rise from his creaking chair and move toward the window. The floor gave and heaved beneath his weight. Seven could see the large shadow blotting out most of the light in the room.

Cy said: "If only you hadn't given him Black Boy. That horse carried you out of some tight places."

"He'll come back," said Delevan, "and – you'll see – the paper will be in his hand and we'll have $400,000 to slice in two."

"Six hundred thousand would make a bigger pile cut two ways," said Storker.

"Don't be a pig, Cy," admonished Delevan, and with those words he bent his body and stuck his huge head from the window. He looked first down the veranda and then back toward Will, staring, as it seemed, right into his face.

Will flattened his legs against the roof and his back against the wall and stared back. Two feet separated their faces as Will held his breath, expecting a startled move from the other. But the light of the room flooding through the opening blinded the fat man, and he could see nothing on either side of the

27

window, but was only able to distinguish objects straight ahead.

As he drew back his head, he spoke: "Funny thing about that kid: I have the feeling he's right here with us; he had a strange look in those light-gray eyes of his when he left us out in back."

"He's long gone from here and you'll never see him ag'in," predicted Storker with finality.

Will wasted no time in creeping from the roof. He left it as he had come – moving without hesitation, like a cat, as he negotiated the porch and dropped to the ground, fading softly into the shadows. He mounted Black Boy and walked the horse quietly from the vicinity of Three Wells, avoiding all contact with other travelers.

With the stars above to guide him and the brisk night breeze blowing into his face, he loped the horse toward the north and west. His gray eyes shone in the dark as he rode along the trail. He laughed aloud on several occasions, a mocking laugh that might have meant anything – had someone heard it.

5.
A Short Trip

Will Seven's course wasn't the truest or the straightest from Three Wells to Gaffert, for that town lay due north. It was ten days' hard riding over rough country from Three Wells to Gaffert; that much Will understood. But since he had never been one to do things the hard way, he headed north and west.

In four hours he intersected the rail spur from Gaffert that ran southwest toward the cattle pens at Union Hill. He paralleled the course of the tracks for several miles and finally stopped in a grove of cottonwoods near Three Mile Creek. Alongside the shining rails stood the dark black silhouette of a water tower. Nearby stood huge piles of cut wood.

He dismounted and waited on the side of the track opposite the firewood and well back in the shadow of the trees. Will smiled minutes later when the melancholy whistle of the Gaffert express sounded far down the track. Next he could feel the ground begin to vibrate as the night train approached. Black Boy could feel it also, for he nervously stamped his feet and pulled back at the bit, a ring of which Seven held firmly in his hand.

Coming around the bend at reduced speed was the locomotive, a 4-4-0 with a great square kerosene reflector-type lamp for a headlight and its funnel-shaped stack spouting sparks. Several coaches in the rear were sprinkled with dim lights. The ruddy, blackened faces of the engineer and fireman could be seen in the light of the boiler fire as they watched from the cab. The engine slid by Will with its wheels screaming as the brakes were applied. The pistons pumped slower and slower as she drew to a stop opposite the water tower, her bell clanging softly in the night. The hiss and sizzle of escaping steam pierced the air as the engineer relieved the boiler preparatory to taking on fresh water.

Two colored men leaped from the forward coach and began throwing cut wood into the tender. The sound of escaping steam, the clanging bell, and the laughing and talking of the engineer and wood loaders gave Will the cover he was seeking. He tied Black Boy securely in the little copse of trees and said:

"Black Boy, I've got to leave you for a minute, but I'll be back – I'd come through hell for you. I'm not goin' to tie anything around your muzzle; that might hurt you too much. Now, you be quiet and don't start squealin' the minute I get out of sight." The horse shivered slightly but stood quietly.

Will darted from the copse in the next instant and reached the rails. In the shadow below the windows of the two coaches he hurried toward the rear of the train. Past the coaches he came to an open hopper car loaded with low-grade ore; next he passed a flatcar loaded with huge logs. Beyond these were three closed freight cars. He tried the door of the first, but it was locked. He hurried on to the next, and found it merely latched shut; he did not attempt to open it, for he could hear the lowing and bawling of cattle within. The next-to-last car was also locked, and as he was getting ready to force it with a jimmy bar he had in his boot, a man stepped down from the caboose, a lantern dangling in his hand.

Will hesitated not an instant, but with the skill born of many years' practice swung under the car and crawled across the rods, and not a minute too soon, for a second man joined the first coming from the caboose. The two men stopped opposite Will and lighted their pipes.

The man with the lantern under his arm said: "Listen, didn't I tell you that damn car should have been up ahead? You can't stick a car crammed to the gills like this one at the tail end of the train with an empty one ahead.

31

Did you feel those curves as we come up through the flat country? Why, I was afraid this car would pull the others off the track."

"Well, Joe," said the other, "we'll know better next time."

"I wish there was a pull-off here," went on the first man. "I'd pull off right now and reverse this car, with the empty one up ahead – schedule or no schedule."

"Well, there ain't no sidin', so forget it," said the second railroader grouchily. "Let's cut through here and go up and have a pull on the jug – now that's the kind of a pull-off I like."

"By Gawd, you like the lightnin' juice, don't you, Bill?" laughed the other.

They passed between the cars.

Will was out and running for the empty car. When he used the jimmy bar on the lock, the long screws pulled easily from the weatherbeaten wood. He slid the door open. The dank, cool smell of the interior flooded out to him. Leaving the door open wide, and glancing about to see if anyone was coming, he dashed back to the woods.

Seconds later he reappeared leading Black Boy, holding the smooth velvet muzzle of the magnificent beast. He paused on the edge of the woods. He could see the dark hulk of the boxcar and the still darker void of the space where the door had been slid open. He led the horse quickly to it.

Will jumped onto the bed of the car still holding the reins, but the horse backed off and clearly would go no farther. Will tugged and cursed, but the strength of the horse was great in spite of the pressure of the bit. After what seemed like painful minutes, he got the animal nearer and succeeded in coaxing it to place its forefeet up on the bed of the car. After much struggling, cursing and cajolery, and with the aid of several lumps of sugar, Will finally succeeded in getting the horse to make the leap onto the low flat bed of the car.

Will wasted no time in tethering the animal at one end of the car; then he turned and hurried to the door. He looked up and down the track, but all seemed to be well. In his excited state he expected an outcry at any second. Should this occur he was prepared to untie the horse and spring from the door, mounting on the run to make a rush for the safety of the cottonwood trees. But no outcry came, and he slid the heavy door closed.

Crouching behind the crack, he awaited whatever might come next. At the other end of the car Black Boy whickered softly. He spoke to the horse in a low tone, and the animal was quiet. Will could hear the men talking near the engine, and he assumed from

33

the conversation, the shouts, and laughter that the job of refueling and taking on of water was nearly done. Presently he heard the two railroaders returning; this time they had evidently crossed over and were coming back on the side of the car with the jimmied lock. He held his breath.

One of the men said: "Say, you're staggerin', Bill. If old Lumely sees you drinkin' on the job – here, I'll help you up there."

"Listen, Joseph, me boy," said Bill, "if I owned this railroad, know what I'd do?"

"What'd you do, old timer?"

"I'd put a barrel of whisky in every car and two in the caboosh, that's what I'd do."

"That's a happy thought," admitted the other, "but old Lumely doesn't drink. I doubt if he'd see things your way."

"Thash right; that old skinflint never bought a drink in his life. All the money he's makin', what good's it doin' him? He don't know what livin' is if he ain't never been drunk."

"There's a heap of truth in that," answered the sober railroader.

They passed the car without noticing the broken lock.

Will pushed some straw into a corner, making himself a bed. As the train jerked the cars taut and started to move, he smiled and closed his eyes. He would sleep now, for he would need his rest. He had cut short the ten-day trip by horseback, and in something over ten hours he would be able to leap the horse from the train outside Gaffert where, somewhere in the vicinity, was Lee Costain and a scrap of paper.

6.
The Whistler

Will stretched and yawned. Though he was stiff and sore from his long rest in the boxcar, he told himself that he had spent worse hours on the road. He inspected Black Boy and found the horse to be taking the trip well. He found more sugar and pressed the sweet lumps to the animal's muzzle; the horse whickered appreciatively. Will talked gently to him above the rumbling noise of the train.

As he examined the animal more carefully in the dim light, his eye fell on the package Delevan had tied on the back of the saddle. He undid the string and opened it. He was about to throw the contents into the corner,

35

for the scrapes he had been through in the tattered garments he wore had given him an odd sense of affection for the rags. However, thinking ahead to Lee Costain, he put aside sentimentality and began to get out of his old clothes.

After donning the new clothing he stepped to the door of the boxcar and slid it open for more light. He found that he had slept through most of the day and that it was afternoon. He surveyed himself. He found that the clothes were not new, as he had presumed; they were, in fact, secondhand, but of fine quality. They had been freshly laundered, for he could smell the odor of laundry soap. The pants were a good fit, blue in color. The shirt was light gray with a fine black stripe. It was the best shirt he had ever worn, and he liked the feel of it against his skin. He threw the string tie out the door, for he had liked a feeling of looseness about his throat ever since a previous experience left him with a feeling of horror in regard to anything tight about his neck.

As he pushed out the crown of a new sombrero that had been stuffed into the package, he noted with a smile the small chain of silver conchas that made up the showy band. He clapped it on his head and drew up the chin string. It too was a good fit.

The boots that Delevan had provided were a trifle too tight, but he surmised that they would stretch, time and Lee Costain willing.

Last of all he strapped on the Colt that Delevan had given him. It was in no way different from any of a thousand others like it except that the front sight was gone, eliminated by some gunsmith to make it come free of the holster easier. He made several flashing draws to test the holster and found that it was no hindrance to him. He liked the gun, and he tossed it about for a minute to get the feel of it.

Seven left the boxcar twenty miles south of Gaffert when the train slowed on a steep incline. He rode the horse out the door, his head held low and close to that of the animal as they shot out of the moving car. They landed in the coarse stone gravel of the roadbed and slid for a moment – the horse quickly regaining his footing and galloping a short distance from the tracks.

A shout from the caboose had greeted his sudden appearance; the two men had rushed out on the rear platform and were yelling and waving their their arms as the train sped away. Will reined in the horse and waved his new hat. The trainmen knew by the way he had ridden the sliding horse in a shower of sparks down the shale gravel bed that the mysterious rider had departed from their train. What they shouted was lost in a blast from the train whistle.

Will turned the black stallion and crossed back over the tracks, heading for the wild country of mountains and rocky valleys north of Gaffert. Two more miles of travel brought him to pleasant farm land and gently rolling slopes sprinkled with patches of virgin timber. In the distance a spread of buildings caught his attention. A neat white farmhouse set back in a grove of cottonwoods appeared to be the main dwelling, while a prosperous-looking barn sported a fresh coat of bright red paint. The fields were patches of color, with one huge section green with winter wheat and another huge patch dull with the stubble of alfalfa in the spring. A third part was freshly tilled brown soil steaming slightly beneath the sun. Through the tranquil scene ran a meandering, sparkling stream that, not far from Will, formed a pool within a pleasant grove of trees. From this grove of thinly spaced trees came the sound of merry whistling. As Will approached and the whistling became louder, he headed Black Boy down the bank into the water and slowly advanced upstream toward the sound.

As he turned the corner he perceived a young boy of ten or eleven sitting on the bank, a fishpole in his hand. He lay on his back with a straw hat tipped over his eyes and his legs crossed. Some noise that the horse and rider made brought a tanned hand up to the hat which at this moment covered his whole face. He lifted up the hat and glanced downstream. One look brought him quickly up.

He shouted: "Hey you – you're riling the stream with that darned hoss! How do you expect me to catch any fish with you using the creek for a bridle path?"

"Are they biting?" queried Will, stopping the horse.

"They *were* biting," scowled the boy.

"What kind are they?" asked Will.

The boy took off his straw hat, revealing a head of twisted curls dark brown in color. He smiled as he began to pull on a stringer that was attached to the bank near him. His smile was puctuated by large spaces between his teeth. He held the fish aloft.

"Catfish, eh?" said Will.

"What's wrong with catfish?" countered the youth.

"Nothin', if you cook them right," said Will, licking his lips.

"Well," said the boy, "my ma can cook 'em all right – if I do the cleanin'." He frowned at remembering this least-liked task of all fishermen – the price of luck.

Will asked, "You live up there in the farmhouse, son?"

"Yep. What are you doin' around here? On the run after a big job, hunh?" asked the boy with a keen glance at Will.

"Me? On the run? No, I'm not on the run. What makes you say that?" said Will, glancing down at himself.

"Well, I just guessed . . . after I saw that bullet hole in your pocket," declared the boy, pointing.

Will glanced down at his pocket to find a small round hole a half-inch in diameter. Inside the pocket he found tobacco and papers, placed there apparently by the foresighted Delevan. He removed the tobacco sack and paper and began to build a cigarette, a smile upon his face at the unexpected pleasure. He found himself wondering to whom the clothes had belonged before him, and shivered a little.

He smiled at the boy, and said: "Son, if that bullet had ever touched me, would I be here talking? That's no bullet hole; that's a – er – tobacco burn is what it is."

"You convinced me," declared the boy with a touch of irony in his voice.

"Well then," Seven smiled, "have it your way. It's a bullet hole all right, but it happened while the shirt was on the line, being washed. You can see that the shirt is pretty clean, can't you?"

"Sure I can see that," began the boy, "and I can also see you ain't from around here. I know everybody around here. Unless you dropped down from the sky, you must have just washed that shirt; you're too far from laundry soap out here to be wearing a clean shirt like that."

"Why?" asked Seven.

"You would have had to come a long way," explained the boy; "you'd be covered with sweat and dust – not fresh as a daisy."

"Well, that's how it happened," said Will.

"Sure," said the boy.

"You know pretty much everybody around here, son?"

"Who you got in mind?" asked the youth proudly.

"A fellow by the name of Lee Costain!" said Will sharply.

"Lee Costain!" exclaimed the boy, paling a little.

"That's the fellow," declared Will, drawing on his cigarette.

"No, I never heard of him," said the boy, looking down.

"I didn't think you would've," said Will with a knowing smile.

41

"No? Why not? What makes you say that?"

"Because you're so young I didn't think you'd know anything important like that!" said Will.

"That's what you think, hunh? You think I don't know what's going on, hunh? You think I don't know any crooks, eh?"

"Of course you don't," said Will, smiling as though he were scoffing at any such idea.

"Well, by gosh, I do know a few crooks, Mister Stranger . . . so take that cat smile off your face. I've heard of Lee Costain and I know where he hangs out. You're a lawman, eh?"

"Nope."

"An outlaw?"

"Maybe."

"You wanta find Lee Costain?"

"Yeah, I'd like to find him. You know where he is, do you?"

"I don't know where he *is*, but I sure know how to find him," admitted the youth with a proud smile.

"How — where?"

"Just keep ridin' back into the hills toward the mountains; they'll find *you* if you get nosy enough."

"How'll I know which trail to take, old-timer?" asked Seven.

"Take the trail to Wolf Canyon."

"And how do I find that?"

"That's easy: watch for a stand of burnt-out pine; that begins the Wolf Canyon Trail. Then just ride up the canyon a ways, and when a rifle splats you out of the saddle – you'll be within a few miles of Lee Costain."

7.
Wolf Canyon

Will splashed Black Boy out of the creek and up the bank. He galloped wide of the farm buildings, turning once in the saddle to wave to the youngster, who had started for home with his catch and fishing gear. The boy waved back.

Seven headed for the hilly country that served as a backdrop for the big farm. He put the stallion to a flying gallop, making use of the even ground and the horse's great speed to cover as much distance as possible before darkness came upon him. He enjoyed the smooth rhythm of flowing motion as the great horse shrank the distance between him and the hills. As he raced along, the wind in his face, his spirits were high, for although he knew that Delevan had lied about the strength of Costain, he also knew that the great train robber was but a mortal like himself. He would go see this Lee Costain for himself and, if the man was too great an obstacle or was too closely guarded, he would merely ride away and forget the paper. Forget the $200,000.

After all, he owed nothing to Delevan, he told himself, for he had heard with his own ears how that fat crook had deliberately lied about Costain. If he rode off with the splendid horse he now bestrode and the $500 as well, that would be a good lesson for Delevan.

But there was always cunning, and with the help of it he might get the paper in spite of the skill and fighting courage of Costain and in spite of the trained and chosen fighters with which he had surrounded himself.

Also, it was true that Costain had never heard of him, and he should be able to go right into the camp of the outlaw without raising too much suspicion. Surely, he reasoned, he did not look like a lawman; one more wandering soul should not arouse too much suspicion. Perhaps Lee would take him into the gang, for was he not mounted on the finest of horseflesh? Then, to his horror, he remembered that Cy Storker had said that Costain was acquainted with the horse.

The startling flashback suddenly caused

him to rein in the horse and look around him. He found himself in the very stand of burnt timber that the young fisherman had spoken of. He glanced back and started to turn the horse, then checked himself and turned the stallion once more toward the mouth of the canyon, and walked the animal slowly into the jaws of the sharp-walled draw.

He could explain the horse in some way – if he was lucky. But what, he thought, if the horse had been stolen from the outlaw? He stopped to consider. He could always say he was returning the horse if that were the case. Hadn't Delevan himself spoken of the superhorse, Bayard, that the bandit possessed? What would a man like Costain want with two such horses? He stopped again, and laughed at the absurdity of his question. He went on, remembering his own poor horse back in Three Wells, which made him think of the old adage among horsemen, "Never become too attached to a horse; you may not be able to trade when a better one comes along."

He had gone some miles into the wild, twisting canyon, thinking thus and arguing with himself. Suddenly a bullet sang past his head, followed by the crack of a rifle. He fell off the horse as though struck dead, and lay still. Black Boy sped forward frightened, but

45

stopped a little farther up the draw and began to graze at the bunches of grass that dotted the trail. Will lay still, not moving a muscle, though his position was a cramped one and his body ached. His heart pounded as he envisioned the unseen rifleman higher up in the rocks drawing a bead for an insurance shot at that very moment. He knew that the slightest move on his part could bring death from a wary marksman who took no chances. Men who took no chances lived the longest; that he accepted as manifest, and prayed that he in the rocks who had just missed was not such a man.

It seemed like an hour, though he knew it to be but a matter of minutes, before he heard a boot scrape on the rock and then, moments later, the slow, shuffling gait of an approaching man. With his head on the ground, tipped back, he squinted barely enough to see the approaching man. The extreme angle of his head made it difficult for him to discern the approaching marksman, but just as he thought he would burst with expectancy the head of the other came into view. As the man approached, more and more of his body was distinguishable until finally, when the man was standing right over him, Will could see the rifle steadily aimed at his heart, and the top half of the outlaw.

The rifleman stared hard at the prostrate form; he was, it appeared, concerned over the absence of blood. He cocked the hammer and nudged Will with the gun barrel. Seven tensed for a last-minute try for his gun, but reason told him to lie still and play dead. If he had brought the man this far into the open, perhaps he could do still more.

"What the hell?" whispered the rifleman to himself. "Musta scared him to death! No marks. . . . Way he's layin', looks like he flew off the horse and broke his neck!" He squatted down, pointing his rifle to the side as he did so, and placed his hand over Will's heart.

Will twisted violently and, grasping the rifle barrel with one hand, smote the man on the side of the face with his free fist. The startled man fell with a cry under the impact of the blow. Seven twisted the rifle free and scrambled to his knees, holding the still warm muzzle against the other's temple.

The man blinked his eyes and frowned, but dared not move from his position on the ground.

"Howdy, old-timer," greeted Seven, for he found the man to be gray-headed and of middle age, though of medium height, thin and wiry.

"I ain't doin' so good, it seems," declared

the upended outlaw.

"I'm glad you ain't careful," said Seven, with a grin.

"By Gawd, ifn there ever is a next time, son, I'll plug you sixteen times before I ever come out from behind a rock!"

"Live and learn, Pop – that's what I say; only, what's the use of me lettin' you live?"

"Plenty," gasped the old outlaw, "if you wanta get out of this canyon alive."

"Seems you weren't aimin' to let me get in alive; how come I should worry about gettin' out?"

"Nobody likes the thought of goin' when the time comes," said the old man, groaning. "You must be one of Costain's boys, hunh?"

"I ain't answering no questions. I don't give a damn what you do; I been tortured by older guys than you."

"The older the better, hunh?"

"With torture, yeah, age is important; you been hurt more, so you've a deal more knowledge of what'll hurt the other guy."

"I wanta see Costain; I've a message for him," lied Seven.

"I can see that you wanta see the chief, damn you; otherwise, why would you be ridin' up this trail like a sightseer, laughin' to yourself, dressed in Sutton's clothes, and ridin' Delevan's hoss?"

"You know those two boys, eh?" queried Will, his senses pricking up at the mention of the owner of the clothes he wore.

"Listen, son, when you come ridin' into my sights with Sutton's clothes on, I made up my mind I was goin' to drop you when you come into range. Then, when you come a little closer and I see the one white stocking on that black hoss and realized he was Black Boy, I got so damned excited I shot you before you was in range, and blew it!" He ended with an exasperated groan, miserable at his failure.

"Well, you can stop worryin' about Sutton," said Seven, taking what he considered to be a calculated risk that the man whose clothes he wore was dead through some doing of the crafty Delevan.

"What? You mean Sutton's dead?" asked the outlaw.

"Look at this!" said Will, poking his finger through the hole in the shirt.

"Right through the heart?" queried the outlaw, a smile coming to his face.

"Dead center," murmured Will.

"That's the kind of news Costain'll read," said the other.

"I've got a little news he'll like," said Will, trying to let the other talk.

"About the hoss, eh? You did for the fat

one too, hunh? Did you get that mean snake
– that Cy –"

"Storker?" interrupted Seven.

"By Gawd, you *did* get them, didn't you?"
exclaimed the outlaw.

"Well, you *might* say I got them, but it
was more of their doin', really," replied Will
truthfully.

The crook grinned. "I knew nobody could
ever get that hoss of Del's without doin'
murder. How'd you get them . . . with a
six-gun?"

"No, a quieter way than that!"

"You sneaked up on them in the night,
hunh?" said the crook, making a slitting
motion across his throat.

"Well, I sneaked up on them, like you say;
but that fat man is strong; he nearly killed
me with one punch," said Will, avoiding any
method of dispatch.

"Ah, well we know how strong he is – and
in other ways too; but it warms my heart to
know he's dead and done for – Cy too, for he
was Delevan's right hand," said the outlaw.

In spite of the fact that Will seemed to have
hit upon the right things to say, thus relieving
to some extent the suspicions of the outlaw,
he nevertheless still held the rifle barrel at the
temple of the downed man. In the distance
they could hear the shouting of horsemen and

the thudding of hoofs. Several riders turned the bend and reined up with a curse, seeing their guard at the mercy of the stranger. The foremost of the riders was a great tall man with straight blond hair that hung down over his forehead. The hair grew thick about his head and tumbled wildly over his ears. His sombrero had flown back off his head in the fierce ride to the scene, and now dangled by the neck string. His features were handsome, if wild-looking.

He shouted: "Hello there. What's up?"

"Keep back, blondie, or your pard here gets a slug in the head," shouted Will.

"Take it easy, stranger," called the tall rider, "though I don't care if you let Harry's brains spill."

"You don't, hunh!" shouted Harry. "By Gawd, you're lookin' at the jasper that let the blood out of Sutton."

"By Judas, he's got Sutton's clothes on," said the tall man, peering at Seven, "but, so what? Sutton had several outfits like that." His hand dropped to the stock of his Winchester, which, it seemed, he was considering drawing out, for the range was too great for a Colt.

"Watch out!" screamed Harry. "He's quicker'n a cat!" It seemed that Harry had read the movement of the other correctly,

51

for with this bit of information the tall rider brought his hand to the pommel of his saddle.

Harry added: "This is Sutton's last suit, Fred; there's a bullet hole right over the heart. This same guy did for Del and Storker, and he's got a message for the chief! Look over there in that bunch of willows. Don't you see Black Boy?"

The heads of the outlaws swung toward the indicated direction, exclamations of surprise and wonder on their lips. An eager rider immediately spurred into the willow copse and came forth leading the spirited black stallion by the reins.

Another outlaw leaped off his horse and ran to the horse, shouting, "It's Black Boy! It's Black Boy!"

"I can see that, you damn fool!" said the man called Fred.

He added, shouting to Will: "What's this message for the chief? I'll take it to him."

"I'll take it myself," replied Seven.

"How do we know you're not an assassin from Delevan?" asked the tall man.

"Del's dead," lied Seven, choking a little at the closeness to the truth of Fred's remark.

"If you're friendly, throw down your gun. What have you to fear?" asked Fred. "We'll take you to the camp."

Harry looked at Will, and his eyes implored

52

the other to do so. He said: "Go ahead, stranger; he means it. His name's Fred Strate; he's tough as nails but he's true: he won't go back on his word. He's straight as they come – around here, anyway!"

Slowly, Will lowered the gun.

8.
Lee Costain

With a shout the riders spurred their horses up and around the pair as Will lowered the rifle. Seven and Harry got to their feet and looked at the circle of riders. The tall man called Fred spoke:

"Take Luke's hoss, Harry, and come back to the camp with us. Luke, you get up in the rocks and stand guard. The boss'll have some questions to ask *you*, Harry, about what you were doin' on the ground here, under this fellow's rifle."

"Then I'll answer to the boss," declared Harry, glaring at Strate.

"You'll do more than answer, I'll wager," said Strate with a laugh. "Give this kid his hoss. Bill, you take the lead back to camp."

He looked at Will. "You go second, and don't try nothin'. I'll be right behind you – you wearer of dead man's clothes, you low-down hoss thief!"

Will glared at Strate, hesitating to mount the horse, for in his heart of hearts he wanted to jump up and drag the long, tough-looking rider from the saddle and give battle. However, he decided to mount up and meet the chief, which, after all, was his main concern, but the insult had nearly brought him into conflict with a subordinate. He smiled mockingly at Strate, and with a salute moved his horse past the leader and fell in behind the rider called Bill.

As they headed up the canyon for a considerable distance, Will could see why it had taken the riders some time to saddle up and come down the canyon to the rescue of the guard. After much twisting and turning, they came to a narrow place in the canyon wall through which they passed to a big clearing. The entrance was only wide enough for a single horse to pass at a time. No wagon could ever have got through the gap. Once through the defile, Seven found himself in a large box canyon off the main trail.

There were clumps of timber standing straight and tall, trying to reach the sunlight above the sheer canyon walls. The floor of

54

the box was covered with thick green grass that Black Boy scented. He bent his head, trying to crop it as they passed slowly down a slight incline, heading toward a large cabin and corral.

The cabin was evidently the present headquarters of Costain, for in the tall doorway, filling the entire opening, stood the giant outlaw, or at least a person that Will would have bet his last dollar was the chief. Will glanced around at the details of the terrain, resolved to examine the place carefully for all means of escape and also to save his nerve for the terrible moment when he must look the giant in the face and not appear frightened. He finished his survey as they approached the corral, confident that there was only one way out of the hideout – the narrow pass through which they had just ridden.

They dismounted, took the saddles from the horses, and turned the animals loose in the big corral where they ran to circle with the large number of excited thoroughbred mounts that were already inside. As in all outlaw camps, each man did his own work, including the lieutenant, Fred Strate; they hoisted their saddles and started for the shed next to the cabin. Inside, Will found a place for his own saddle and, glaring contemptuously at Strate as he passed, walked out into the open.

The rest of the men stood around, awkwardly casting glances at Will. Harry walked to his side as he stepped out of the shed. A moment later Fred Strate came through the doorway and joined the group, glaring at Seven as he came up.

The long, lanky form of Costain ambled toward them from the cabin. "What's this fellow doin' here, Fred? What's Harry doin' here? Where's Luke?"

"Luke's out on guard," said Fred.

"But it's Harry's turn," protested the chief. "Who's this guy?" His ugly features twisted into a great frown.

He was close to them now, and Will could see Costain in all his fabled hugeness. It was true that he was six and a half feet tall – thin, but rangy and rawboned. His face was an ugly sight, half of the skin being bright red – scalded, the story went, in a steam explosion on one of the trains he was robbing. A great, hawk-like nose split his face, and the ridge of it appeared as sharp as a hatchet. The other side of the face presented a deep-sunken cheek crossed by a livid scar that traveled from mouth to ear and back across to the eye, giving the impression that the triangular patch had been lifted up at some time in a horrible fight. His ears were huge, with gigantic lobes

56

hanging down in the fringes of his touseled hair which was a sandy red.

When he opened his mouth he revealed huge horse-like teeth. Enormous, sad eyes looked out over this terrible countenance and took Will Seven in. It was almost as though the beautiful, expressive eyes begged forgiveness for the face, Will thought as he met the stare of Costain. He found that he could meet the eyes as long as he did not look at the horrible face. Even the pale-skinned forehead that was at the moment pile on pile of wrinkles was a hard thing to gaze upon.

Will spoke: "I'm Will Seven. I'm the guy you've been looking for, Costain. I'm the guy who can keep somebody from cashin' in on that reward on your head!"

"You are?" asked Costain.

"I am. You need protection, and it's plain you're not getting it here. Didn't I ride right in here?"

"That seems to be the case," said Costain, glaring at the other men.

"Why, I could snatch out my Colt and put you on my list right now," said Seven, snapping his fingers and making several of the outlaws start.

"Who's on your list now?" asked Costain.

"There's Sutton," interrupted Harry, holding up his hand to tick off the victims

57

on various fingers, "and there's Delevan and Storker, for three. I was almost Number Four – out there in the canyon!"

Costain jumped as though stabbed. "Del's been done for by this kid? Seven is your name, eh? And Storker dead – I can't believe it! By Gawd, Harry, how'd this kid ever get the drop on an old-timer like you?"

"Well," said Harry, relishing the spotlight, "when I see this kid coming up the draw on Delevan's hoss and wearing Sutton's clothes, I says to myself, 'Oh, oh – here comes Sutton for the chief's scalp, and it looks like he's done for Delevan!' I thought that because he was riding Black Boy."

Costain nodded. It seemed logical to him also.

"Then," continued Harry, "I got nervous as he jogged along in my sights, comin' into range, because he was laughin'."

"Just a minute," interrupted Costain. "You say he was laughing as he rode up the trail?"

"Right out loud," said Harry. "Anyway, I had him cold turkey, but I slipped or something as I pulled the trigger, because my shot never touched him."

"How come you didn't shoot again?" asked the chief, unable to understand how one of his men could have failed to do something so important.

58

"That was the good part," admitted the outlaw. "The kid here, he tore backward out of the saddle like he had a holt on a cannon ball. He plunked down in the dust and never moved a muscle. He looked gone to me, and I thought my shot had gone home. I tiptoed down, keeping him under the bead of the rifle all the time, and so help me he never moved a muscle. He was all balled up too, in a hell of a position. So help me Gawd, before I knew what had happened he actually grabbed my rifle and nearly broke the side of my jaw with his first swipe at me. That's how it was, Chief – that's square. I was a damn fool for being suckered like that, but the fact that the kid took me in proves he's good. When did I ever let you down before?"

"Never," admitted Costain, rubbing his jaw and looking at Will.

"Aw," began Strate, "I say he's a spy – maybe a damned Pinkerton. That's probably how he got Sutton and Del."

"You spoke the main thing, son, when you said you could jump out your blaster and cut me in two," said Costain, speaking directly to Will.

"We'd cut him down," threatened Fred, scowling.

"Sure," said Costain, "you'd cut him down after I was gone. You might better save him

59

for his brains – the lot of you sure ain't got any."

"Why, you could split him in two the best day he ever lived, Chief," scowled Fred.

"How do you know?" asked Costain, looking at Will. "I think myself I could, but how do you know? Could any of you have taken Del in a fair fight? This kid has a look in his eye. Look at him. He ain't scared to die. He looks like he's ready to go to hell right now. As for me, I'm not. Let him be. He says he's the man that can take a hold on things for me, and maybe he is. Besides, he can't get out of here alive; so let's give him room to show us something. If he's done all the things Harry says, he's welcome to sleep in my camp. If he hasn't, I'll find out!"

"But he got me to bring him in here because he says he's got a message for you, Chief," protested Fred. "Now he seems to have forgot it."

Will cursed himself as he remembered. Of course there was no message, at least none that Costain would have been willing to hear. Will whirled on Fred Strate, going to the big blond rider and saying: "Listen, you big lug. I've had an earful of your talk. Now shut up or I'm gonna cut you down to my size!"

Fred Strate gasped, for this was strong talk before the others.

Will looked up into the face of the other; there was a good four inches of extra height that the blond man enjoyed over him.

Fred looked exasperated at Costain, and said, "Have I gotta take that kind of talk?"

"I don't interfere in fights in this camp, Fred; you should know that," said the leader.

"Apologize, runt, or I'm gonna tap you on the head and make a fence post out of you," snarled Strate, raising his fist menacingly.

"Oh, yeah," growled Seven, raising up on his toes.

"Yeah."

"Well, go ahead and take the first punch; hit me right on the chin here, will you? Go on, give it a good belt, you big blond baby!" offered Will.

"You want me to hit you first, Seven?"

"Yeah."

"Well, runts first. Make your start."

"All right, big boy, but first move away from that tuft of snake grass; you might use that for an excuse and –"

"What tuft of snake – ouch!" Fred never got the chance to finish, for the uppercut caught him flush on the nose as he looked down. He sank with a groan to the ground.

The outlaws howled and danced at the sneak punch, for they expected the lieutenant to come off the ground filled with fighting

61

fury, as did Will himself. But Fred sat on the seat of his pants and held his nose, groaning with pain. The fight was over.

As he removed his hand from his face, Lee Costain jumped forward and said: "Hold it, Fred! Your nose is busted clean loose. If you get tagged there again, the pain'll kill you!"

Fred nodded, for he seemed to concur with his chief.

9.
Doctor Costain

As Will stood looking at the fallen lieutenant and the other outlaws, he spoke: "Anybody else want to make somethin' of it?"

The rest of the men glared at him, but they made no answer and seemed content to shift their feet about in the dust and stare at the ground.

Costain glanced up from the spot where he knelt at Fred's side. "The boys have seen enough of your ways, Seven. You've shown them a few tricks – what with your performance out in the canyon and now here in camp. That was as good a sneak punch as I ever seen throwed."

"It wasn't so sneaky," declared Will.

"No," began the chief, "perhaps it wasn't. Let's just call it a tricky blow. Don't misunderstand me, kid. I've put a few fellows to sleep with a well-timed first punch. But I don't know as I ever used the finesse that you just showed – getting a guy to look down into an uppercut like that!"

"It was nothin'," said Will modestly.

"Oh, it was more than nothing, eh, Fred?" asked the outlaw leader, looking at the nose of his lieutenant.

"Like bein' kicked by a horse is nothin'. That's the kind of nothin' it was!" said Fred, his eyes rolling with pain.

"Come and get it!" yelled a man from the cabin door.

For some time Will had been aware of the odor of cooking coming from a cabin nearby. Now, with the fight finished, for the time being, he began to realize that he was ravenously hungry. The smell of food seemed to abate his hostility, and he wondered if it had not had some effect upon the others as they shuffled toward the cabin.

A bearded, squat man in a greasy cook's apron scowled at them from the doorway and yelled: "Well, are yuh comin' or ain'tcha? I'm gettin' sick of cookin' for this crew. If it ain't a gunfight then it's a fist fight. An' when it ain't neither of them it's somebody breakin' a bronco. You guys can go to hell – I quit. I'll be damned if I'll cook food and then let it get cold. Cook yore own grub from *now* on!" The cook disappeared into the shadows of the cabin, trailing a string of invectives regarding the profession of cooking for fighting men that made Will smile.

Costain glanced up from the ground where he was attempting to stem the flow of blood from Fred's nose with his handkerchief. "Go ahead and eat with the boys, Seven, I'll help Fred along here. We'll be right behind you; we'll attend to this nose after supper. Good cooks are hard to find for camps like this. It's hell to cook and then have people not come to eat." As the outlaw chief helped the other man up, he continued:

"How about it, Fred? Can you eat supper all right?"

"I think so," responded the other, getting to his feet slowly.

"By Gawd, I knew you could!" cried Costain proudly. He smiled at Will, and said: "Fred here can eat most any time. He loves to eat, drunk or sober. He even eats when he's wounded!"

"That takes a good appetite," admitted Will as they walked to the cabin together.

Confidence left Will in a rush when he stepped through the door of the cabin with Costain and Strate. The inside was lighted by several flaring kerosene lamps, and two long tables seated all the outlaws in the camp. The cook and a boyish-appearing helper served the food on great platters. Outside, in the dim light of dusk, the men had not appeared so formidable, but now, in the glaring artificial light, they seemed different. A stiff twilight breeze was blowing through the open doors and windows, causing the lanterns to sway a good deal. As the light rose and fell on the grizzled, scarred faces of the outlaws, it revealed them suddenly as a pack of wild wolf-men, snarling and growling as they gulped the food placed before them. Will thought, as he stood awkwardly waiting for some direction from Costain as to where to sit, that only the formality of the table and benches separated the men from being mere animals.

They pushed and shoved with their elbows as they greedily went after the food, grabbing up whole joints of meat and snapping and tearing at the roasted flesh as though they were ferocious beasts. One whole table seemed to be the jostling mass of some multiheaded monster that was devouring everything in sight and would, if the supply of food ran short, support itself by cannibalism and begin devouring its own limbs next.

An argument broke out as two men reached for a single remaining piece of meat, and the two contestants leaped to their feet and began slugging toe to toe. Will blinked as the blows landed, splatting with such force that he thought quickly back to his challenge in the yard of a moment before, and regretted having made it. The two combatants ceased as suddenly as they had begun when a new platter of freshly cooked meat was put on the table by the cook's helper. They went back to the table with a joyous shout and reached for their share of the meat. Many hands flew with theirs, and the platter was almost cleaned as forearms and hands darted in and out, wiping the meat and gravy on each other's shirt sleeves.

"Twenty fellows like this must build up a big meat bill," said Will, glancing at Costain.

"Beef is cheap," said Costain with a grin.

Will guessed the significance of this remark, but he remained perplexed as to where the three of them would eat. Costain ended all speculation when he stepped toward the nearest table and, wedging his hands between two of the eaters in the middle of one of the long sides, swept the men tumbling along the bench as though he were scattering empty dishes from a shelf. The outer men fell cursing to the floor as the chief opened up this huge hole in the ranks. As Costain climbed over the bench, he motioned for Strate and Seven to join him.

They clambered in beside him, Will noting the sullen looks that were thrown their way, but no man dared to curse at the giant chieftain. Following the example of the others, Will shot out a hand and grasped one of the joints of meat; as he did so he perceived that several hands of the outlaws shrank back from contact with his own. This amused him, for he himself was afraid of these very desperadoes that were shrinking from him. He devoured as much of the roasted beef and steak as his belly would hold, telling himself that he might have to sustain himself with this meal for many days to come.

One by one, their appetites quelled by the tremendous glutting, the outlaws began leaving the table for chairs and bunks within the room. They smoked pipes or rolled cigarettes, and began an after-dinner grumbling and belching that reminded Will of a pack of lions he had once seen fed in a zoo back East. Several large pots of steaming black coffee were spread around the tables, and the men drank innumerable cups to wash down the meal.

Costain had drained his eighth cup – Will had counted them unbelievingly – when he at last turned to Strate. Fred had, in spite of his painful impairment, consumed nearly as much beef and coffee as had the chief.

"Fred," began Costain, "something has to be done about that nose."

"What can be done about it?" queried Fred, his voice now having a peculiar nasal twang. "He can't take the punch back out of my nose and put it in his fist, can he?"

"No, haw, haw, haw," bellowed Costain, slapping the table, tears rolling down the scarred cheeks from his expressive eyes.

Will smiled in spite of his fear of the chief, for tears were human whether they came from laughter or grief, and whatever was human he admired. He found he admired Lee Costain.

The chief continued: "That beak should be set, Fred. Otherwise you're goin' to look like me!"

"That *would* be hell," admitted the handsome Strate, glancing at the hook-nosed chieftain.

"I seen a doctor set a nose once," declared Costain.

"You think you could set mine, eh?" asked Fred doubtfully.

"Why, yes, I could have a pull at it," said

68

Costain, nodding his head.

"A pull!" exclaimed Fred, making a frightened face. "You ain't gonna *pull* on it, are you? Listen, Lee, nobody's gonna pull on this nose – not after the way it's been *pushed* today." He glared at Will, who looked down at the table.

"With a *sort* of pull is the way it's done. First you pull it up and then you lift it over," said Costain.

"Does it hurt?" moaned Fred.

"Anybody I ever heard of having it done claimed that it hurt like hell," said Costain truthfully.

"Then forget it," ordered Fred.

"Look, Fred, you're a good-lookin' guy. Why, you're handsome; your looks have plenty of class, and they've helped the gang more than once, haven't they? Your looks took us by some big stumbling blocks, remember?"

"Yeah, I remember those girls – but I don't like that kind of work."

"I don't like that sort of thing any more than you, but look how it helps at times. We'd never have got the news of this money shipment if you hadn't romanced the station-master's wife. Besides, she wasn't a bitter pill to swallow, was she?"

"No, she was pleasant work," admitted

Fred, smiling at the memory.

"Besides, it might affect your breathing."

"How?" yelled Fred, jumping up. "Is that a threat – is that all I'm good for around here – my looks?"

"I'm not threatening you, Fred," said the chief, his voice calm. "I'm just stating a fact. Any of the boys here with a busted beak can tell you that it's true. When your nose has been broke and not fixed proper, it can make it hard to breath at times – especially when the seasons change."

"Is that so?" asked Fred, glancing around the room at the others, who had grown quiet listening to the conversation.

"Yep, that's a fact," said one man.

Several others with hawk noses agreed with nods and comments that this was true.

"How'd you do this operation?" queried Fred.

"It ain't no operation – maybe I can't even do it – but I'll give it a try," admitted Costain. "Just climb up on the table and I'll see what I can do."

The cook's helper had most of the wreckage of the meal cleared away, so Fred, casting a doubtful glance at the chief and a glare at Will, who had brought all this trouble, climbed onto the table and lay on his back.

No sooner was he down than the others

started from their places and ringed the table, staring down at the victim. Costain and Will stood up.

10.
Setting Things Straight

"It looks like I've died an' gone to hell," murmured Strate, looking up at the circle of faces. "Looks like I'm ringed in by a bunch of devils."

"Let's see now," began Lee, rubbing his hands to get as much of the grease of the meal as possible from the surface of his fingers, "first we should have some antiseptic. Whisky is good for that. Somebody get a jug."

Almost immediately a heavy earthen jug was set on the table near the chief.

"Now," went on Costain, "we need something to drug the kid with – to keep down the pain."

"Let's cancel this," said Fred, sitting up. "We ain't got no drugs here!"

"Take a pull on this jug," ordered the chief. "That's as good as a drug."

71

"Funny as hell," murmured Fred, taking the jug to his lips.

He gulped for a minute, and the quantity of whisky that he swallowed amazed Will and brought applause from the other onlookers, for such feats were very admirable in their eyes. He lowered the jug and sat for a minute, a ludicrous expression beginning to play about his mouth, and this, with his bent nose, made him look very odd indeed. With a sigh he settled back and looked at the ceiling, his eyes bleary.

Costain turned to the crew that surrounded the table.

"Let's see, now; who's the best whittler here?"

"To hell with this!" yelled the bleary-eyed Fred, sitting up, only to be restrained by many hands at a glance from the chief. "Let go, you scum! Let go of me! Nobody's goin' to whittle my nose into shape. Lee, you said you'd pull it!"

"Quiet," ordered Costain. "Nobody's going to cut your nose. I want somebody to make a sort of splint for after I get it set!"

"A splint, eh?" said Fred, settling back under the outlaws' hands.

"Sure, a splint. Now, I think Harry is about the best whittler we've got," added the chief.

"Harry can whittle a beautiful horse," volunteered one of the men.

"I don't want no nose that looks like a horse," growled Fred.

Costain ignored this remark, though it convulsed Will and most of the others.

"What does a nose splint look like?" asked Harry, stepping forward and snapping the blade out of his clasp knife.

"Well, I don't rightly know," admitted Costain, rubbing his craggy chin. "I never seen that part of the operation done, but I suppose that if you carved a sort of socket that was shaped on the inside like this nose used to be, that'd do the trick."

"That's easy," declared Harry. "Let me through there to have a look at that nose." He pushed his way through the men and stared at the swollen profile of Fred's nose. He held his finger before his eyes, making measurements which he quickly committed to memory.

"You remember what it looked like before, don't you, Harry?" asked Lee, seeming very concerned.

"Yeah, I remember it. It was nice and straight then. I'm just getting the bulk of it now."

He stooped down and glimpsed Fred's profile. He left the group, then, and went to

73

the fireplace, where he picked up a piece of white birch and immediately began to carve. His knife was sharp, and the keen edge sent chips and slivers flying as he started the job.

"Put about six holes in it, and we can tie it on," ordered Costain.

"Now we'll need some packing for this nose," added the chief, "for it's goin' to bleed a good deal when we're done. Which of you boys has something clean? A good clean piece of cloth is what we need now!"

The outlaws looked quizzically at one another, for it appeared that they owned very little that was clean.

"I've got a little something," said a voice finally, after a long silence.

The chief, looking at the outlaw who had spoken, said proudly to Will: "This is a great gang. Somebody always comes through at the crucial time."

Will nodded.

"What is it, Bob?" asked the chief.

The man had left the group and was now coming toward them with his saddle bags. He glanced around at the others and put his hand furtively in the bag. Slowly he brought out a clean silk cloth.

A gasp came from the men present.

"My Gawd, what's that?" asked Lee.

74

"It's a petticoat," said one of the men hoarsely.

"By Gawd, that's what it is!" declared Costain. "Where'd you get this, Bob?"

"What the hell difference does it make?" bristled Bob, growing red in the face.

"Why, it don't make no difference – if you got it off a clothesline. But Fred here don't want nothin' like that in his nose if you – well . . . it would be bad luck for him if you –"

"That's where I got it – off a clothesline," admitted Bob.

"We'll use it, then," said the chief, smiling.

The chagrined Bob left the room to the laughter and jeers of the outlaws.

"Hurry up, damn it," moaned Fred. "I don't give a hoot where he got the cloth as long as it's clean. Get on with the job."

"Okay, I'm ready to go to work," said Costain, and grabbing the jug he tilted it up with one arm and let the amber fluid trickle down his throat. He held the jug there for a long while.

"Hey," yelled Fred, looking up, "hey, don't get drunk! Gimme that jug!"

Strate grabbed it away from the chief and started to drink himself.

"I thought you had enough," said Costain.

"I did until I see you startin' to get stiff,"

growled Fred. "But if you're gonna operate drunk, I'm not gonna lay here and take it sober." He gulped some more and finally settled back, holding his burning stomach.

"I was just steadyin' my nerves," said Costain.

Well, I'm just paralyzing mine," Fred informed him.

"Are you ready, Fred?"

"Pull away. I can't feel a thing."

"Hold him, boys!" yelled Costain.

The men gripped the startled Strate as Costain bent to the task at hand. Taking hold of Fred's head with one hand and grabbing his nose with the other, he wrenched down and then up.

A tremendous scream filled the room, causing several of the outlaws to go white. Some of those at the rear ran out the door rather than watch any more.

"Is it done, Lee?" groaned Fred.

"No, I missed my hold. It slipped off when you jumped so. Can't you other fellows hold him tighter?"

He glanced at the circle of pale faces around the table. At the sound of the terrible scream Will had thrown both his arms around the flailing legs of the mighty Strate, and he still held the grip, pinning Fred's limbs against the table with his chest.

"We'll try. Go ahead, Lee," said Will.

"I'm gonna lift this time," declared the outlaw. "Get set. Now!"

Another horrible scream pierced the stillness of the cabin, and one of the outlaws, feeling faint, walked to his bunk and fell down. Those outside rushed in and looked at the intent circle of faces. Pale as death, the outlaws held their fierce grips on Strate and looked to the face of Costain, which had gone white except for the livid scar on one side.

The chief was holding the nose firmly by the bridge and staring at his work.

"It's straight!" someone murmured.

"Is it done?" gasped Fred, blood streaming from his nose.

"It's done," declared the chief. "By Gawd, I *actually* did it!" He still held the nose and smiled at the others who, gazing with great reverence at their leader, relaxed their grips. "Tear the clean cloth into narrow strips and I'll pack the nostrils with it."

This was quickly done.

"Here's the splint," said Harry, proudly offering his carving.

"By gosh, it fits right over his nose like a shoe," said one of the men admiringly.

Costain completed the surgery by tying the nosepiece in place with a quantity of string.

Fred sat up and looked around at them.

"By Judas, he looks funny!" said Harry, laughing.

"He'd look a sight funnier without it," said Costain.

"It don't hurt at all!" said Fred, amazed, "I'm numb."

"That's good, old son," said Costain, "because we've got to start makin' the final plans for the holdup. The time has been set for the shipment. Clear this stuff off the table and get out the maps and things!"

11.
Plans Are Laid

The lantern light fell softly on the maps and papers that were spread before Lee Costain. He had rolled up his sleeves, revealing thick, heavy wrists covered with hair. To Will his scarred face was a study in horror as he sat before them and scanned the map. The others had drawn their chairs and benches close to the table that the chief occupied. He had hastily rolled a cigarette and, with some of Fred Strate's blood still on his hands, smoked and waved his arm about as he made known his plans.

Fred was lying on his bunk, his eyes riveted on the ceiling. His nose splint had brought forth some derisive comments from the rough crew and caused him to give some dark looks in return. Now he avoided the group, though he listened intently to the conversation at the table.

"This is the Gaffert Road," Lee said, pointing at the map. "This is the spot where we drop two of you boys off to flag the train."

"What good'll that do?" asked someone. "The train won't stop, will it?"

"Sure it will," declared Lee, glancing up. "This is the one spot where the train can be flagged – people from Mosby do it all the time. They ride down here to the Gaffert Road, and where the road crosses the tracks they flag the train."

The chief scratched inside his open shirt collar, and as he did so Will's heart leaped, for the string around his neck was visible. Will wondered about the string and the paper: suddenly he was much more attentive to the plans for the train robbery.

"I've flagged the train there," nodded one of the men.

"Good, Art. You and Harry can slip on at

that point. That'll give us four men already on the train."

"Four? How does that give us four?" asked Fred.

"You and Seven can get on as regular passengers at Cleary. Nobody up there knows Will –do they, kid?"

"No," answered Seven, "I've never been to Cleary."

"And you ain't never gonna be there, either," yelled Strate from his bunk. "I ain't travelin' with him, Chief – that's out!"

"You've got to, Fred," answered the leader. "We can cover that nose guard of yours with bandages. That'll hide most of your face – a perfect disguise."

There was a low murmur of approval.

"What's his share in this?" asked Strate, sitting up.

"He splits equal if the job comes off – after my share off the top, of course. What's wrong with that?"

There was silence.

"I see," murmured the chief, looking around at them. "You don't trust the kid 'cause he ain't never ridden with us, is that it?"

There was no answer.

"How many of *you* did I trust on the first job?" continued Costain. "Fred, did I ever doubt you after you threw in with me? Haven't I been able to pick out the spies? Did I ever make a mistake? Besides, you'll be right with the kid all the time. Are you afraid of him?"

"No, I ain't afraid of him," growled Fred.

"Good. Then you keep your eyes on him; but unless I miss my guess, he'll be worth two of you in the pinch. He's already proved that as far as I'm concerned. Who else has anything to say against Seven here? What, all quiet? Then I guess you've changed your minds about him, hunh?"

The room remained silent.

"How much is in the shipment?" asked someone, changing the subject.

"Not too big a haul," answered Costain: "a little over $100,000. It's not enough for us but that's why we're striking. They won't expect me to take such risks for $100,000. But three or four easy jobs like this, and we've picked up half a million. I'd just as soon do these easy jobs as I would one big tough one."

"How about the guards?" asked Art.

"Only six of them: Joe Becker and his two brothers and three other deputies!"

"Holy cow! The Becker brothers – they're poison," said one of the men.

There was a chorus of affirmative remarks concerning the Becker family.

Costain whirled, facing the man who had first spoken. "What'd you expect? A tea party? Maybe you think they put a ribbon and a thank-you note on $100,000 cash, eh?"

"Naw, I didn't think nothin' like that," said the man.

"Well, listen, Doby; I don't like the way you think. I hate it when somebody throws the towel in before a job even gets off the table. If you don't believe a job can be done, forget it. That's my way. Now, I know Joe Becker and all the crooks he's been poison to. But I don't hold no fear of him. There's six of them and near to twenty of us. That's winning odds. The rest of the people on the train can't be counted on to give us any trouble – they're all yellow."

"Joe Becker ain't much," said Harry. "He's mean as hell, but that ain't nothin' to fear. He's a dead shot, just like his brothers; but, like the chief here says, we'll have them outnumbered and outgunned."

"We'll surprise the hell out of them, getting on in the middle of the tunnel like that." Costain laughed, throwing back his head and revealing his huge horse-like teeth. So great was the exertion of his mirth that his shirt collar widened and a small pouch was visible.

Will stared at the string and pouch that contained the paper worth $600,000 to

Delevan and Storker. Will wondered why the paper wasn't worth an equal amount to Costain.

"I don't think this has ever been tried, do you, Chief?" asked Harry.

"It's a new idea with me," admitted Costain, "and it's one thing Joe Becker will never think of in advance. I can just see the look on his honest face when we step into that car!" He ended with a shout, the humor of it convulsing him, as it did some of the others.

"I'd like to be there and see it myself," said Art. "Where you gonna shoot him, Chief? Where you gonna drill him – between the eyes?"

"No," said Costain, his features distorted still more horribly by the humor of the thought, "I think I'll give it to Joe in the guts!"

Will shuddered involuntarily.

"I can see his face," said Doby, grinning. "I can just see his face – Gawd, ole Joe will be surprised!" He stopped suddenly and looked at Will. "Hey," he said, "the kid ain't smilin'. He don't think it's funny."

This sobered them. They stared at Will.

"What'sa matter, kid?" asked Costain. "Can't you see the joke?"

"No."

The room fell silent.

"Why not?" asked Costain, his voice growing ominous.

"Gut-shootin' is too good for Becker. He oughta be dragged!"

"You mean hoss-dragged, eh?" asked Costain, considering this new idea.

"No, I mean train-dragged," answered Seven with a cold smile.

They studied the kid, but no one laughed or spoke. Several put their hands to their throats; others slowly rubbed themselves in various places, no doubt thinking of the jolting type of death Seven favored for his victims.

"That *would* be a hard way to die," nodded the chief, his features devoid of laugher.

Costain put away the papers, for they had been over the main scheme a dozen times before. Tonight they had merely settled the manner of getting a quartet of men onto the train. The train schedule they all knew. Only Will didn't know how the main body would board the train in the middle of the tunnel; it was information they wouldn't give him.

Will spent a restless night thinking of what was ahead. Lee Costain slept not at all, but paced back and forth, awakening the men for their watches and welcoming back those who came in from their shift. Will could see that the price of $20,000 on his head was a source of great unrest to the outlaw. He pondered how he might slip up close enough to get the pouch off the neck of the crook.

Twice he started up from his bed, as slowly and as quietly as a cat. A quick dash and he could tap the chieftain over the head with the butt of his Colt and tear the string loose. He could expect to make it as far as the corral without a hitch, but what luck he'd have catching up Black Boy he did not know. It would be dark, and perhaps he would be discovered before he could get a bit in the horse's mouth and a saddle on its back. Once mounted, he would have a hard ride to get clear of the band, but he might do it.

Each time that he started up from his blankets, however, the form of Fred Strate also sat up in bed. Finally he fell asleep cursing Delevan and Storker.

He cursed again in the morning when he found that he and Fred were to leave at once for Cleary. He turned in the saddle and waved to Costain as they entered the narrow defile that led from the outlaw camp. Now his only course would be to go through with the robbery and try to get the pouch with its paper afterward. Besides, he was curious as to how the job would be accomplished by the outlaws.

As they rode through the country south

85

of the mountains, Will decided that if he were to learn anything about the method of getting on the train it would not be from Fred Strate, for he ignored all attempts at conversation.

They made a camp in the flat country outside Cleary and ate the provisions the camp cook had given them. Again it was a restless night for Will as he worried about Strate, and the outlaw was also suspicious of every move on the part of Will.

The next morning they rode into Cleary and bought tickets for the trip to Gaffert. Strate was disguised, with his head swathed in bandages. They left their horses at the livery stable where, Strate informed Will, another man would pick them up the next day. This had all been arranged by Costain.

As they boarded the train at ten-thirty and took their seats, Will got his first look at Sheriff Joe Becker. He was a big, good-looking fellow with crossed gun belts. He had dark curly hair and a good-natured but hard smile. He came through the train talking to the passengers and looking everyone over. He passed Fred and Will to converse with an older man in the seat ahead, the only other passenger in that car.

"Mornin', Mr. Wilson. Nice day for a trip, eh?"

"Yes, Joe – very nice. Er, is everything all set?"

"As set as you can get with $100,000," said Becker.

"Sh-hh, quiet, man, quiet!" groaned the older man, glancing back at Will and Fred.

"Aw, it's all right, Mr. Wilson: just a couple of cowboys takin' a train ride. Looks like that one fellow busted his head in a bad fall from a bronc."

"Just the same . . ." said Mr. Wilson.

"Listen Mr. Wilson, your money is in a box, and do you know what's around that box? A big strong safe. And sitting right around that safe, like it was a warm stove in January, are my two brothers and three other crack shots. And do you know what they got with them? Ten shotguns. Ten rifles. Twenty Colts. All loaded and ready for fun. Besides, the door to the express car is locked and bolted at both ends and in the middle."

Will nudged Fred.

"That sounds reassuring. Still, don't go blabbing in front of every yokel you see," cautioned the old man.

"Listen, Mr. Wilson," declared Joe Becker, "even Lee Costain hasn't got a chance at this shipment. We've" – he lowered his voice so that only those very near could hear . . . "We've got a man in the cab watchin' up

87

ahead. We've got a man in the caboose lookin' out for the rear. We've got a man on top! Yep, ridin' right on top. He'll be up there the whole trip – except when we go through the tunnel, of course."

"I think I'll go forward and take a little nap. It smells like horses here," said Mr. Wilson, glancing back at Fred and Will. "You've relieved my mind a good deal, Becker. I'll remember your thoroughness." He rose from his seat and went forward, Joe Becker accompanying him.

12.
"Gold Don't Fly Far!"

Will glanced at Fred.

"What you gapin' at?" asked Strate.

"Did you hear that?" asked Will, referring to the conversation. "They've got six crack shots and forty loaded guns – and three other fellows hidden around besides. How in hell does Lee expect to overcome odds like those?"

"We've got 'em outnumbered; and as for the guns, you don't think we're short in that department, do you?" answered Fred, and he patted his vest to indicate that there were more firearms hidden there in addition to the big iron on his hip.

"How about this Becker? He looks like he'll be strong in a pinch."

"You weren't worried so much about him the other night. You said you was gonna train-drag him!" reminded Fred.

"He's a big fellow!" admitted Will. "I don't think I could get a rope on him."

"He'll stand still for Mr. Colt," laughed Strate.

Will noted that there was not the slightest trace of fear in Fred's voice. It seemed rather that he was becoming more and more alert and happy as they approached the mountains and the tunnel. At the moment he was sitting with his head on the back of the seat and his hat tilted over his eyes, humming a pleasant tune. He was obviously delighted with the prospect of the coming bloodshed.

"How does Lee get on the train?" asked Will, nonchalantly.

Fred raised his hat and looked at the other quizzically.

"Well, there ain't no harm in tellin' you now," he murmured. "You can't get off the train and do anything about it." He shifted around in the seat so that he could face Will

89

easier and raised his hat above his eyes. He continued:

"Lee and a dozen of the boys are in the tunnel, see?"

"They'll be killed," declared Will, hoping to draw more of the plan from Fred.

"No. We dug a pocket right in the side – there's plenty of room for them *and* the train. When the engine goes by – at reduced speed, of course, because there's so many rock slides in the tunnel – the boys will just slip on all along the length of the train. When we hit daylight, Costain and the rest of the crew will be swarming all around us. We'll kill the guards outside the express car and stop the train. Then we'll uncouple everything from the express car back, and some of us will take the engine and the rest of the cars up the tracks about five miles. Gahagen will be waitin' there with a whole line of horses; we'll let all the water out of the boilers and bring the horses back here to Lee."

"We'll shoot our way through the Becker brothers, eh?"

"No, you fool; we'll just dynamite the car to hell. If Becker don't want to surrender, he's hash!" Fred laughed.

"Won't dynamite hurt the money?" asked Will.

"It's gold, stupid. Gold don't fly far!"

Fred settled back with a chuckle and dropped his hat over his eyes once more.

Will stood up suddenly, and at the same time lifted Fred's hat.

"Hey, what the hell you doing?" asked Fred with a startled look.

"I'm lookin' for the right spot," said Will, smiling.

"Gimme my hat – what spot?"

"This spot right here!" snarled Seven, and smacked Strate alongside the skull with the heavy barrel of his Colt.

Strate's head dropped limply to the side as he sagged into unconsciousness with a groan. Will replaced the hat and pushed the limp form closer to the window, where it could lean against the wall of the car for support. He hurried forward toward the engine. He passed through the next two cars without incident, but groaned as he was leaving the second of the two, for ahead of him was the large form of Joe Becker.

"Howdy, cowboy," said Becker with a smile as they faced each other in the small passage. "Where's your sidekick?"

"Oh, he's back sleepin'," said Will.

"Where you goin', cowboy?"

"Just walkin'," said Will.

They both looked up as the whistle of the

train blew shrilly.

"What's that mean?"

"We're coming to the tunnel is all." Becker smiled. "Don't look so worried, friend. The engineer will cut this speed to nothin' before we hit the tunnel. You been on trains before; I can see that."

"Listen, Becker – that's your name, isn't it?" asked Will hurriedly.

"Don't shout. I can hear you fine."

"I've got to get by," snarled Will, and tried to dive through the space between the wall and the big lawman, but Becker reached out and dragged Will back by the shoulder.

Seven glanced down at the savage grip on his shoulder and up into the eyes of Becker. The softness he had noted was gone.

"Listen, you fool!" Will warned. "I'm tryin' to save your life!" He twisted free and glared at the sheriff.

"You're gonna save my life, eh? How you gonna do that?"

"I've got to go ahead," shouted Will above the roar of the swaying car.

"There's nobody up there in that car," advised Becker. "Just a couple of cowboys that flagged the train at the Gaffert Road."

"That's Art and Harry – two train robbers!" cried Will.

"Train robbers, eh? Them two ain't gonna

92

do any business on this train!" Becker laughed.

"They're just two of four already on the train, you fool!" cried Will as the whistle shrieked once more.

"What?" yelled Becker.

"And twenty more are jumpin' on in the tunnel!" continued Will.

"Twenty! Oh, my Gawd – in the tunnel? Twenty-four's too many for us – but if we can kill the other four first . . . Where are the other two?"

"I'm one," admitted Will in his excitement, forgetting what the implication would mean. He blinked, for the two guns of Joe Becker had flashed from their holsters and were trained on his heart almost before he had finished the words.

"Freeze!"

"I'm stiff," declared Will. "But look, Becker, I'm not in on this deal all the way. If I was, would I have tapped Fred Strate on the head and come up here to warn you?"

"Fred Strate! Is he the one with the bandages on? Is Fred Strate the fellow that was with you?"

Will nodded.

"Then that means that Long Lee –"

"– Costain is doin' this job," interrupted Will, finishing the sentence for the lawman.

"What the hell are you in this for?"

"I want a few minutes alone with Costain," answered Will.

"You do, hunh? An ambition like that can kill a guy – specially a little one like you!"

Will stared at the other. "My God, Becker, are you gonna stand here all day and chat?"

"This is as good a place to wait as any." Becker holstered his guns lightly.

"I've got a better idea," said Will.

"Spill it," said Becker. As though he had nothing better to do, the lawman took out the makings and began to build a cigarette. He spread his feet and braced himself against the sway of the car.

"We'll go up ahead and speed up the train – can this wood burner go faster?"

"Sure, but we can't take a tunnel at this speed."

"Why not?"

"Rock slides."

"Hell, Becker, use your head – Costain would have them all cleared up. He wouldn't take any chance on the train having to stop in the tunnel. Lee is depending on surprise when you fellows come blinking into the daylight with the sun hurting your eyes!"

"That makes sense; but we'll have to shoot this Art and Harry to get through to the engineer and tell him to pour it on!"

94

"Do we have to shoot them?" asked Will, taken aback at the callous attitude of the other.

"Why not? If they get the chance, they'll shoot us!" was Becker's logical answer.

"We could tie them up," offered Will.

"Listen. Anybody that would crave to be alone with Costain won't be squeamish. I'll plug those two and tell the engineer. You go back and shoot Fred Strate. He's so fast with a gun that if he learns the double cross you're pullin' he'll fill you full of lead while you're thinkin' about drawin'!"

"All right," said Will, undecided.

"See you in a minute or so," promised Becker confidently. He turned and started for the door.

The train was starting to slow down.

Will went back through the car. When he was halfway to the other end, gunfire broke out in the car that Becker had entered. Will froze as a dozen shots rang out, punctuated by curses and howls of surprised rage and pain. He turned and raced to the aid of the lawman.

As Will dashed through the door with his pistol drawn, to his amazement he found that Art was on the floor – dead. Harry was sitting in the aisle with his back against a seat; he had both hands clutched to his breast, but the blood was gushing through his fingers. He was dying quickly. As he glanced at Will, and choked, "Traitor!" a large bubble of blood broke on his lips. He fell forward, dead.

As Joe Becker passed out the door at the end of the car, Will noted that he was stuffing shells into his guns as he went. Becker apparently had been hit in the shoulder, for a stain of blood was evident on his shirt. He disappeared, and Will turned and raced back toward the car where he had left Strate. He feared that Fred had been roused by the gunfire.

The passengers, huddling together like young birds, looked up, alarmed anew as he went running down the aisles. He reached the car and burst through the door only to be met by the startled Mr. Wilson who, it seemed, had an interest in the money that was on board.

13.
Train Robbery

"My God! What's up? Where's Becker? Did I hear shooting?" queried Wilson, as he stepped out of Will's path.

"Train robbery!" shouted Will.

The words seemed to bring Fred Strate out of his daze, he lurched erect, groaning and holding his head.

"Is it time?" he croaked, his voice a hoarse whisper.

"Yes, it's time again," said Seven, knocking Strate on the head once more.

The outlaw fell back again. Will pulled some rawhide from his pocket and began lashing Fred's hands and feet.

Wilson ran up. "Young man, is this fellow one of the robbers?"

"Yes," said Will without looking up from his work.

"What happened to Becker?"

"He's up ahead – speedin' up the train."

"My God, we'll all be killed in the tunnel!" groaned Wilson.

"No danger of that," advised Will, finishing the bindings and standing up. "Lee Costain just cleared the tunnel. That's where he's gonna hop aboard."

"Lee Costain! My Gawd, what good's money if you're dead?" howled Wilson, wringing his hands.

"Shut up. We're gonna save your money! Sit down here and keep this fellow from getting loose."

"Yes, sir," gasped Wilson, dropping into

97

the seat and staring at Will.

Will left him and raced for the front of the train. He could feel the cars lurching and swaying under him at greater speed now, and as he ran down the aisles the passengers viewed his third appearance with even greater alarm, for they connected it with the increased speed of the train and the shots.

He yelled: "Sit down and be quiet, folks! Everything is gonna be all right – just keep calm."

Through an open door ahead he could see Joe Becker sitting on the wood in the tender, talking to another man. The lawman was intent upon stuffing a bandage inside his shirt. He looked up and smiled as Will came through the opening.

"Howdy," he greeted. "This is Rip Roth." He indicated the lookout who had been stationed in the cab.

Will nodded. "How fast are we goin'?"

"I don't know, but we'll have to slow down plenty for that sharp curve inside the tunnel. Some of them may be able to climb aboard, but not many!"

"It'll be some surprise," admitted Will. "Still, I'll bet Costain will make it aboard." Will glanced ahead at the mountain and the curving tracks that led straight into the dark hole of the tunnel.

"How many do you think'll get on?" asked Will.

"Maybe four!" predicted Becker, with a broad smile at the thought.

"Remember, if we get Costain alive, I get to spend a few minutes with him," reminded Will.

"You'll get your minutes with him. That's a promise from Joe Becker." He smiled when he said it, as though the promise meant a great deal to him. "Did you kill Strate?"

"No."

"What?" he gasped, leaping up.

"Get down," yelled Will.

"Don't order me –"

"We're comin' to the tunnel," screamed Will, pointing ahead.

Joe Becker cursed, and looked around. He ran into the first car with Will. Roth drew his pistol and remained at the back of the tender, poised and ready to start shooting the minute the train came into the daylight.

"Hurry!" screamed Becker, racing for the express car.

As they dashed past the startled Wilson, who sat obediently holding Strate erect, Will saw that Strate was conscious and staring wild-eyed at the running pair.

"Open up. Open up! It's me, Joe! Open the door, damn it!" screamed Joe, pounding on

99

the door of the express car. As he pounded on the door and tried to make himself heard above the roar of the train, they were suddenly plunged into darkness.

"Open up! Open this door in the name of the law!" screamed Becker, forgetting that there were nothing but lawmen inside.

"Go to hell," came the faint answer from inside. "Joe Becker told us not to open this door come hell or high water – until we get to Gaffert Station."

"Gawd, they don't recognize my voice," moaned Becker, looking back at Will. "Open up, you damn fool!" screamed Becker. "Don't you recognise your own brother's voice?"

The answer was a bullet that tore through the heavy door. Will and Joe stumbled over each other as they raced back into the next car for safety.

"The damn fools – they're sure doin' what I told them," groaned Becker. "I can't understand why they can't make out my voice!"

"It's the roar of the train in the tunnel," said Will.

"Well, there's only one thing to do: you and I'll have to climb up on top and meet them when we come out of the tunnel. We sure ain't gonna get any help from those deaf fools in the express car. Too bad: five of the best shots in the county all sitting around playing poker while we gotta go out and trade slugs with Lee Costain and his gang."

They stood at either end of the car, waiting for the train to come to the end of the tunnel. Will thought that the darkness was fading and becoming a deep gray. Up ahead in one of the other cars he could see that the conductor had lighted some of the lamps.

Suddenly the sunlight flooded about them once more, and Will noted that Becker had climbed from sight. He grasped the iron bars and began pulling himself upward. He could hear gunfire forward on the train, and in the last second before they had emerged from the tunnel there had been a long, horrible scream from outside the train. Evidently the outlaws were having trouble boarding the train.

As Will turned his head, he saw an outlaw struggling in the narrow opening between the cars to hold the footing he had won and at the same time draw his gun. Will placed both hands on the railing and kicked out with his boot. The outlaw cursed and grabbed at the foot to block the blow. Somehow he fired his gun as he got hold of Will's boot, only to lose his hold and tumble off the train. The shot that he fired went wild, and a piercing scream was the last that Seven heard of him.

Will's heart was beating wildly as he started up the ladder once more. This time he got all the way to the top, and as he glanced forward he saw that four outlaws had made the roof of the cars and two more were struggling up the side, trying to make the catwalk. Joe Becker was grappling furiously with one of them.

Becker's lookout in the caboose came up his ladder only to be shot in the side of the face by one of Costain's men. Will watched in horror as the lookout, with part of his face blown away, drew his gun and killed the outlaw who had shot him. Costain's man tumbled from the top of the caboose.

Will crouched on his hands and knees to keep from falling from the train, which was now hurtling and lurching along at high speed. He could hear Rip Roth screaming and cursing as he fought his way forward in a crouching position, his gun spitting orange flame. Roth shot two of the outlaws dead as he came forward; then the tall, lean form of Lee Costain went running toward Roth. Will could see Costain's long red hair flying in the wind. There were more flashes of gunfire as the two faced each other at the length of a car; then Roth went stumbling to a horrible death between the wheels.

Costain whirled and came racing back

toward Joe Becker. Will heard a bullet sing past his ear. Costain screamed something at Will as Seven raised his gun from the holster. Costain fired, though the range was great. Will heard a shout behind him, and looked back in time to see the lookout on the caboose falling from the train – shot at a distance of three passenger cars by Costain.

For the first time since the awful moment when he saw Costain raising his gun, Will realized what had happened. The outlaw leader had saved his life, for the lookout hadn't known Will from any of the other outlaws. Costain had shot the lookout in an attempt to save the life of one of his men.

The huge outlaw's face was distorted with rage as he fired at Becker and the sheriff fired back. There was a pause as both men discovered their guns were empty; then Costain rushed in for the kill. He caught Becker with a great kick, doubling the lawman over. Then they closed, with Costain striking fiercely with his Colt and Becker holding up his hand to shield himself, having thrown the useless gun aside, believing that the outlaw would do the same. As Will started to run forward, he came abreast of the remaining outlaw.

"Hold it, Seven! The chief'll handle Becker. Where's Fred?"

103

"Down there," yelled Will, and shoved the outlaw off the train. Will saw him hit the rocky edge of the roadbed and roll over and over, only to bounce miraculously to his feet and stand dizzily watching the end of the train roar by.

Will raced forward. Becker was hanging from the top of the car, and Costain was kneeling on the catwalk, holding his gun by the barrel and laughing like a maniac as he pounded the fingers of first one hand and then the other of the lawman with the heavy butt of the Colt. Will rushed up and grabbed him from behind, around the throat, and used all his strength to drag the choking outlaw away.

14.
All Square

"Let go! What the hell, Seven!"

Costain flung a long arm back and smashed Will in the jaw; then both hurtled apart as Will released his grip. Costain whirled with a savage snarl and hurled himself toward Will. The outlaw chief knew that something had gone wrong: the train had come through the tunnel at too great a speed; Fred Strate was not in evidence in the fight; Joe Becker and his men had been ready for the fight. All these things pointed to the one unknown quantity present – Will Seven.

With all the hate that he held for the railroads within his soul, with all the rage he contained because of the accident that had scalded him, with all his hatred of man and society he drove at Will. Had his hate not been so great, had his face not been such a cyst on his soul, perhaps he would have aimed his flying attack better. As it was, he hurtled through the air a foot too high, knocked his adversary to the roof, and let out a great scream as he slipped over the edge, grasping frantically to hold on.

Will scrambled to take advantage of the turn.

Strangely, he found himself screaming and prying at the fingers of Costain, trying with all his heart to kill the other. Suddenly he looked into the face of Costain. It wasn't the face of a sane man, he thought, and yet as he looked into the eyes filled with hate and at the flaring nostrils and twisted mouth something changed inside him. He could see the neck muscles of Costain corded and straining as he fought to hold onto the top of the car. Then Will saw the string within his reach, and leaned out and took hold of it.

As he did so, the eyes of Costain bulged. In that instant, and from that gesture, he guessed everything about Will Seven. Will saw him go limp and start to sag; he realized that the strength was going out of Costain's body.

Will jerked on the string and felt it break and come free. He stuffed the string and pouch into his pocket and settled back to watch the outlaw fall from exhaustion.

The cords in his neck were bulging to the very extremities of his loose collar as Costain fought the losing battle. His face had turned almost blue; his eyes were popping out of his head. His hair blew into his eyes, blinding him. His fingers were red streaked with white, revealing the horrible strain of holding up his great weight.

Slowly his head sank lower, in little convulsive jerks, a half-inch at a time. Once he fought back up a little, and Will tensed to fight him off should he by some miracle gain the top. But he quickly sagged even lower, and presently his head was not visible to Will at all. Still the fingers clung stubbornly to their precious grip. Will marveled. He looked over the edge. Costain was doggedly clinging

106

– hanging by his fingers at his arm's length, swinging in the wind.

Will reached down, grabbed the wrist of the outlaw, and began to pull with both hands. At this first contact Costain looked up unbelievingly. Then he nodded and released the other hand, clawing with his fingers and nails at the side of the train to give Will any help he could. Then Costain, still possessed of great strength, took hold of Will's leg and began pulling himself in hand over hand, and finally crawled to the top just as the train started to slow down.

They both sat exhausted, drinking in huge quantities of air and choking and gasping for more. Will held the gun loosely, covering the chest of the chief.

Costain nodded the thanks he was still too exhausted to speak.

As the train stopped, Will could hear the excited conversation of the passengers below. Joe Becker came running along the catwalk again with a freshly loaded Colt, blood streaming from his shoulder and his clothes ripped and torn from his fight with Costain and the other man.

"Nice work! By Gawd, we licked them good! You got Lee yourself and saved my life, and that much I won't ever forget. There's $20,000 on Lee's head, and you get it all – er

– what's your name?"

"His name is Seven, Will Seven," muttered Costain, "and he's good luck for me, Becker. He just saved my life too!"

"Well, Seven, the folks in Gaffert are gonna be awful glad to meet you. Why, you'll be a hero there, there's gonna be a big dance tonight, too. Now you get your five minutes alone with Costain. I keep my word. I'll just step down the car here and turn my back for five minutes," said Becker, taking out a battered watch.

"Never mind, we had our chat while I was pulling him on board," advised Will.

"That's funny," began Joe; "you both seemed too out of breath to do much talkin' when I got here!"

"Well, you might say that we came to a mutual understandin'," said Will, winking at Costain.

"We sure did," snarled the crook.

"Say, look over there," pointed Becker. "Here comes a gent leadin' a whole line of hosses."

"That'd be Gahagen, Becker. Those are Costain's horses. Put your hands up like you was stuck up – put up your gun."

Becker complied.

"Wave him in, Lee; stand up and wave him in," panted Will, waving his Colt.

Costain stood up and waved Gahagen toward the train. The outlaw hesitated and approached warily, driving the horses before him. Presently he was sufficiently in range to make himself heard.

"What the hell's wrong, Chief? The train went ripping right past me – express car and all! I had to run the hosses like hell to even follow you!"

"Listen, Becker," began Will, "this is where I leave you. I'm gonna go down there and take one of those horses. I've got business in other parts. Besides, some of Costain's boys are still around. This ain't gonna be no picnic grounds for me. If you're serious about that $20,000 – stick it in the Gaffert Bank in my name. I'll drop in some day when I'm down on my luck and pick it up."

"You can't just walk out of here like this, Seven. I don't even know who you are. Why, you gotta come to town for one night anyway!" said Becker, scowling.

"I'm goin', Joe. It's been nice knowin' you," said Will. "Besides, this is the only way you can get those horses down there, because that fellow Gahagen is gonna get awful nervous if we don't answer him pretty soon. You wouldn't let a guy get away with all of Costain's horses, would you?"

"Oh, all right, Seven, but I still think your part in this is damn funny. How do I know you're not wanted? You were friends with all these guys."

"If you even find out that I am, keep the $20,000," offered Will.

Becker grinned.

Will waved at Gahagen. "Stay out there a minute," he yelled.

Gahagen could be heard cursing.

"So long, Lee," said Will with a smile as he started for the ladder.

"We're even, kid," grunted Costain. "I picked that guard off your back just as he was gonna drill you, and you saved my life and squared things. Next time I see you, remember that."

"Try to," called Will from the ground.

Will hurried out to Gahagen and looked up at the mounted outlaw. He spoke: "The boss wants you in there pronto, Gahagen, everything is goin' wrong!"

"The hell you say. I wrangle the hosses – you go back!"

"Better hurry up," said Will, turning and waving at Costain.

The outlaw chieftain shook his fist back at Will.

"Gawd, he looks pretty mad," groaned Gahagen, dismounting.

110

15.
New Business

Delevan loved the barbershop, and spent a great deal of time there. He liked a good haircut and he enjoyed the luxury of a hot towel and a good close, clean shave. When a good establishment was nearby, he almost never shaved himself.

His ponderous bulk was at this moment tilted back in the chair, his countenance swathed in a steaming towel. The barber was saying, "That too hot, Mr. Delevan?"

"No, Pete – that's just fine; you're a great hand at this, Pete. Bet you learned in New York, eh? Never ran across many men out here that were much with a hot towel. There was a fellow in Philadelphia that I once knew –"

"I got a brother in Philly," said Pete, working up a batch of lather.

"You've told us about your brother's shop a dozen times," complained a loafer, throwing down a battered magazine. "You gotta tell us about him ag'in? We all know about his big shop with *five* chairs."

111

"Six," corrected Pete, scowling at the man.

Suddenly a tremendous boom shook the whole building. One of the loungers jumped up and ran to the window, not in alarm, but as one who had expected the blast but nevertheless felt compelled to inspect the source of it.

"Twelve o'clock," murmured Delevan, his great body jiggling slightly as he chuckled inwardly.

"Sure is a great idea of yours, Mr. Delevan. Folks around here can set their clocks by that cannon of yours. Don't that powder cost you a lot, though?"

Delevan stretched out and crossed his feet. "Why, no, Pete. The whole thing is advertising you see. Since I rented the old Sheldon place for a gunshop, if I want to attract trade I've gotta come up with something that will make people know me and – more important – remember me. This cannon popping off every day at noon is my trade-mark you might say. People can set their watches by it. We check the time every day, and I can say that she goes off just like the big steam whistles blow back East."

"Sure does shake things up," said one of the men sitting about the room.

"Well, I haven't been able to think of any

112

way to shoot that cannon quietly." Delevan laughed.

One of the men snickered. "Mr. Delevan, that big cannon of yours not only has the town on its toes but a lot of the ranchers can hear it go off too. Why, I was standin' down by the bank the other day, and I hear Mr. Elgin say that he could hear her way out to his ranch in the valley."

"You mean you was loafin' down by the bank, don't you, Ed?" sneered the other loafer.

"Loafin'! Whata yuh mean, loafin'? I was down there on business, if it's any news to you!" said Ed.

"Business! What the hell business have you got with Dan Elgin, hunh?" said the other.

"I didn't say I had business with Dan Elgin. I was just standin' near there on business is all. What business would Dan Elgin have with me? That old skinflint wouldn't lend money to the Bank of England! He guards the money in that bank of his like a mother eagle."

"Now, boys," said Delevan from beneath his towel, "don't be unfair to Dan Elgin. He's a sharp businessman, I'll admit, but he's fair. Why, he lent me money to go into business and he rented me the Sheldon place at a fair price. There's $5,000 worth of guns in stock over there now. He lent me that

113

much. But boys, the interest was mighty high – 6 per cent!"

The others whistled.

Delevan continued: "But it's worth it to me. I like to keep my own cash in a liquid state, as they say." He sighed.

"Mr. Delevan, I'll tell you something," offered Ed.

"What's that?" asked Delevan.

"If you hadn't walked into the bank and deposited a big sack of cash like you did, Dan Elgin wouldn't have loaned you $5,000. As a matter of fact, he wouldn't even have rented you the Sheldon Place. Somebody said there was $20,000 in that black bag of yours."

"Well, by God," yelled Delevan, from under the towel, "somebody lied, I'll tell you! There was $25,000 in the bag. That damn Elgin can't hold his tongue, eh? By God, I'll take my money out of that bank – in due time. For the present it's as safe there as it would be in my room. Safer, I suppose, for I've heard that Elgin runs a neat shop!"

He sighed and settled back. The other two men and the barber stared at one another, for they had never heard him raise his voice, and the amount of his deposit startled them too.

"Why does a feller like you, Mr. Delevan, borrow money – when he's got a stake like you have?" asked Ed, his face perplexed.

"Business, Ed. Just sound business – always work on the bank's money when you can. That way they're beholden to you. See what I mean?"

"That's a kind of business I can't get the hang of," admitted the other with a frown.

Delevan chuckled, delighted with this answer.

"Well, Ed, someday you'll see that it can turn a big profit in a way that you never dreamed of. Just wait and see if time doesn't prove me right."

"Here comes Storker," advised the barber.

Storker entered the shop and glanced around. It was evident from his dark look at the loafers that he was disturbed by their presence. Under his arm he had what was a fresh, for that periodical-starved location, newspaper. He sat down with a sigh, folded the paper across his knee, and pretended to read.

Delevan spoke: "That you, Cy?"

"Yeah."

"How's things over at the shop?"

"A shambles," said Storker.

"Oh, how's that?"

"Oh, you know how it is when that cannon goes off outside. Dust gets all over from the recoil. I have to dust that damn place nineteen times a day!"

115

"Well, it keeps us from being idle, and that's something," said Delevan.

"Got the newspaper off the stage," said Storker, rattling the pages so the man under the towels could hear.

"Is the stage in already?"

"Yeah, it's in," said Storker.

"What's new in the world?"

"Oh, the same old stuff. Country goin' to get in some war over in Europe. Some guy here says we should stay out of it."

"He's right," murmured Delevan. "What else is new?"

"Well, most of the space here is devoted to the big train robbery up in Gaffert."

"Oh, how much did they get?"

"Nuthin'," said Cy.

"Who robbed the train?" asked Ed. "Was it Long Lee Costain, ag'in?"

"Yeah, it was Long Lee; only, he didn't have his usual luck this time. He ran into a little trouble – fellow by the name of Will Seven."

"How's that?" asked Delevan, pulling the towel tighter about his face.

"Why, this fellow Seven is a regular hero up there in Gaffert. Seems Joe Becker and he single-handed brought down the whole Costain gang in one big loop. Says here that Fred Strate was taken captive along with the

116

rest of them. Says Becker's account of the capture gives all the credit to Seven."

"Who is this Will Seven?" asked the barber.

"Gawd, that name has a ring to it," declared Ed.

"It seems," continued Storker, "that Seven won the confidence of Costain and was in on the planning of the robbery – a little over $100,000 was the price of the party. Then the story goes on and gives all the details of the way they planned to take the express car – would have worked, too, if this Seven hadn't given Becker a warning. When they had to slow down in the tunnel, that's when Costain would have bought tickets for all his boys."

The others laughed, leaning forward in their chairs.

Cy continued: "This Seven, he puts the slug on Fred Strate and hog-ties him; then he goes and gets Becker, and the two of them decide not to let the other guards in on the party; they decide to take on fifteen – the two of them! Well, two of Becker's guards learn about the thing and they join in at the last minute, but they was both shot. Seven and Becker fight most of the crooks off just like they was at sea and keepin' a bunch of pirates from boardin' a ship. They get pretty well through the bunch of them when Costain

117

almost nails Becker. But Seven comes running to the rescue and fights Costain to a finish."

As Cy paused for breath, Delevan ripped the towel off his face and stared, waiting for the rest.

"Well," continued Cy, "this Seven, he gets Long Lee hangin' from the edge of the train, after giving him a good sound thrashing, but he ends up by hauling the crook back on board and saving his life!"

Delevan fell back into the chair with a groan.

"How could anybody around here get the better of Costain in a hand-to-hand fight? Why, that face of his would scare most people to death. How could anybody fight against a face like that?" said Pete.

"Seven ain't from around here," explained Storker. "Then they couldn't even get him to come into town to a hero's welcome. Seven has a few words with Costain and hops off the train right then and there. They beg him to come into town and get the $20,000 reward that's ridin' on Costain's noggin, but he trusts Joe Becker to put it in the bank in his name."

"I'd trust Joe Becker," murmured Ed.

"It also says that Costain and Strate will get forty years apiece for their work the last few years!" read Cy.

"That seems like a fair amount of time,"

said Delevan, under the scraping razor of Pete.

"When did all this happen?" asked Pete, wiping some lather from the razor.

"Must'a' been yesterday," said Delevan, his voice muffled.

"Was a *week* ago," said Storker with emphasis.

"*A week!*" screamed Delevan, jumping up in the chair.

"Oh, now, Mr. Delevan," complained Pete, "you made me nick you when you jumped like that!"

16.
Return of a Hero

The old Sheldon place was well suited to being a gun-shop. The experienced Delevan had carefully examined the building for every possibility before he decided to open up. The gun shop, he thought, was an excellent idea, for it lent credulity to his use of the cannon to signal twelve o'clock each day.

With the help of the handy Storker he had constructed gun racks around all the walls, and now he had the place lined with rifles and shot guns. In the glass cases that once had housed other goods he had stored every conceivable type of hand gun. The shop was already the second most popular spot of the menfolk in town, the barbershop attracting only slightly more idlers and loafers than did Delevan's Gun Store, as it was called.

Delevan had not hesitated in his buying of stock. After all, as he had told Cy Storker, the bank was lending the money and a good front was important. In the long run it would cost them nothing. Besides next to robbing banks, and sitting under hot towels and eating, Delevan loved to be around guns. Therefore, when he laid in the stock of weapons, using Dan Elgin's money, he had been careful to choose many fancy weapons.

There were carved stocks that many gun fanciers would envy, and there was a choice of engraving work that would have left many gun collectors nervous wrecks had they tried to make a choice among them. Now Delevan and Storker were diligently wiping the dust from the rifles and guns, using lightly-oiled rags. As they worked they talked, taking the guns one by one down from the racks and running the oily rags over the stocks and gleaming blue metal parts. Delevan spoke first.

"You've probably been right all along, Cy – about the kid, I mean. Still, I had faith in him. I was sure he was square."

"He's square, all right; he nicked us with a corner, he's so square. I tried to tell you, but you know it all! What do we do now? Without the paper a *miss* is as good as a mile."

"That's true," murmured Delevan. "Well, there must be a way without the paper. Maybe I can get Elgin to take me down to that vault of his again. Still, with that damn labyrinth –"

"That's the thing that's got us licked," began Cy. "If only you could remember the way it went. When I was down there I got so turned around I didn't know north from straight up. He's a tricky devil, that Elgin."

"The damn thing of it is," said Delevan, taking down a shotgun and sighting along the barrels before he started to dust it, "that we can be sure of where it is within fifty feet; but underground and in solid rock, fifty feet is like fifty miles."

Storker sighed, nodding his head.

"My hands are so damn sore I can hardly hold these guns," he said, looking down at them.

"Well, if Seven has flown, like you say, your hands are in for a rest, my friend."

"There ain't no 'if' about it, Del. You were

121

suckered by that kid. You just helped him to $20,000 by showing him where Costain was; and you had to throw in the best horse west of the big river to sweeten the deal, and $500 cash besides!"

Delevan glanced at the other. "Cy, you don't need to talk like that. You don't have to raise your voice to me. As for the money, why I'll square that with you. I'll give you your half of it right now." He reached for his wallet. "But just give this a little thought, Cy: the kid is in on the deal, see, a $100,000 hoist with a split sure to give him $5,000. Not $500 – $5,000 gold! It sounded like a good plan that Costain had worked out, but one thing killed it – Seven. If he was just going to skip, he would've waited until after the gold was split up. Therefore I say the kid never thought for a minute to blow on us. Something went wrong, and made him go in on the holdup. . . . Probably he couldn't get close enough to Lee any other way.

"You heard that he had a moment alone with Costain – or that that was what he had requested. A word about what? Why, the answer is as plain as the nose on your face. The paper, that's what they talked about. I say the kid got hold of the paper without Becker knowing it, and of course Lee wouldn't say anything."

122

"Aw, that's nuts – everything points the other way!" exclaimed Storker.

"Nonsense, Cy," retorted Delevan. "Use your head. Would Will leave the care of twenty grand to Joe Becker? I don't care how honest Becker is – that tramp ain't gonna trust anybody for $20,000 unless –"

"Unless what?"

"Unless he stood to gain ten times that much!"

"Two hundred thousand," multiplied Cy. "Why, of course – his share of this job!"

"That's it precisely," said Delevan, beaming. "Seven knew that if he went into Gaffert and waited around for the reward some hitch might develop. It could be just a technicality or it could be in the form of Costain's boys that are still on the loose. He's smart, Will is. He got clear, quick! Why he's not back I can't say. He made a lot of friends with that play of his. 'Put it in the bank,' he says. By God, that statement was made for you and me, Cy – for our ears alone. He meant that if this job fails, he'd go back and collect the reward after the heat was off."

"I hope to hell you're right. Put your wallet away. I'm not worried about the measly handout you gave the bum – oh, oh, here comes Dan Elgin across the street. Looks like we're gonna have an official visit."

"Humph," grunted Delevan. "I wonder what he wants. I sure hate to see a banker comin' in the door. There's just something about it –"

Dan Elgin stepped through the door, causing the bell that was attached to it to ring, and smiled at them.

"Busy at work, eh, Delevan? Er – hello there, Storker, God, it sure is dusty in here."

"Well, the recoil of that cannon kicks up a lot of dust out there in the street. Then, too, this old place wasn't too clean when we moved in. The vibrations shake a lot of dirt down from the beams." He glanced up at the ceiling.

"Ah, yes, that damnable cannon stunt of yours. I've been meaning to ask you about that. How much of the loan I gave you had dribbled out the end of it?"

"Why, your money went for stock, Elgin, every cent of it. You must be able to see $5,000 worth of guns about the walls here."

Elgin nodded his head.

"Okay, okay, I just wondered. Still, that cannon seems wasteful and, for that matter, to be causing you a lot of extra work."

Delevan smiled. "Well, don't worry about that part of it. This dust can't last forever. We'll get this place cleaned out sooner or

124

later, won't we, Cy?" asked Delevan, turning to his partner.

"I'm sure of it," said Cy. "This morning I didn't think we'd ever clean the place out; but now I'm sure of it." Cy glanced at Delevan and let his eyes wander slowly out to the street.

Delevan followed the sly movement of the other's glance to the hitch rack before the store. He contained his pleasure, though the window showed a scene that delighted his heart – Will Seven dismounting from the big black stallion and knocking the dust from his clothes with his hat. The youth stared up at the sign, and smiled.

Dan Elgin also turned and looked out the window. He exclaimed: "Why, that's the tramp – and by God he's got your horse! I thought I hadn't seen that horse around the livery stable! Delevan, what's behind this: that no-good with your horse?"

Storker glanced panic-stricken at Delevan.

Delevan smiled happily and burst from behind the counter, brushing past the perplexed Elgin and meeting the boy at the door.

"Will, my boy! You've come back to take the job, eh? By golly, you can't believe how happy this makes me!"

Seven punched the hand of Delevan aside

and scowled at Dan Elgin. "Sure, I can see that you're tickled, Del, but what's this egg doin' here? He's the guy that had me beat up!"

"Why, you insolent tramp," began Elgin, staring at the boy, "what are you doin' here? I'm not lending money to anybody that has you in their fold!"

"Just a minute, Elgin, you do this boy an injustice. He's a hero, you know."

"A hero? For what? Stealing horses? Brawling in the street? For what is he a hero?" demanded Elgin.

"He's Will Seven!" exclaimed Delevan proudly. "He's the fellow that saved the day for Joe Becker up near Gaffert. He's the lad that took Long Lee Costain by the scruff of the neck and shook him until the law laid its hands on. He has $20,000 in the bank against a rainy day! Not bad for a lad in his twenties, eh, Elgin."

"You're Will – he's Will . . . what? My boy, I'm glad to make your acquaintance. I knew you had drive that day you thrashed my crew. I said to myself, 'Here's a boy that's going to make a name for himself.' I know character when I see it. So you've got the reward money in the bank in Gaffert, eh? Tut, tut, too bad. That bank's not safe. I know the place that Bradley runs – rickety – very rickety, my boy. Better get that money down here; have it transferred. Better still, I'll transfer it for you. Say, I could give you a special deal on interest, too." He winked at Will.

Will stared back.

Elgin stood smiling at the boy, but his face gradually began to change, as though some thought that he had not considered had just come to him.

Storker stood frozen in his tracks. He stared at Elgin, anticipating what was coming.

"Wait a minute!" exclaimed Elgin. "What the devil *is* this? The kid here rides up on *your* horse! How come he's on your horse, Delevan? There's something mighty funny about –"

"The funny thing is," interrupted Delevan, "that Will here got to a sentimental old fat man when he was in town last. That's the funny thing, Elgin. I'm a businessman. And I call myself sharp, but the sight of this kid scrapping in the street with your boys did something to me. You've got to admit that Will put up some fight, and won. Well, that sort of got me thinking as I watched them. 'Here's a kid,' I said to myself, 'that's got all the grit a man needs, but what else has he got? Nothing,' I answered myself. Then I thought back to when I was his age. I remembered a dear friend that picked me out of the street and gave me my first break.

"You won't believe it, Elgin, but I saw myself in this youth. I thought with a little help he might really turn into something. And when he jumped out of the dirt and licked that crew of yours, I resolved to reward him by giving him a decent break, for I could see that decent breaks were something he hadn't been getting."

Delevan paused to let this last remark sink in.

"I had him up to the room after the fight and I gave him Black Boy. Gave him the horse outright! Damnedest thing I ever did, Elgin: gave away a $2,000 horse to a stranger I hadn't known but an hour. Did it on a hunch. I do a lot on hunches."

"You gave away a $2,000 horse – I can't believe it!" gasped Elgin.

"That's only part of it," smiled Delevan, warming to the revelation. "I gave him $500 cash to boot – just to help him to something better. Cy here thought I was crazy."

"Is that the truth?" asked Elgin, turning to Cy and then to Will.

Will smiled, and spoke: "It's the truth, mister. Del, here's your $500 back." He handed over five $100 bills.

Cy choked, growing red in the face.

128

Delevan held up his hand, protesting the return.

"Take it," ordered Will. "Take it or the deal is off. If you still want me to take a job with you, you gotta take the money."

"All right, Will, I'll take it," sighed Delevan, and he pulled his pocket handkerchief from his pocket and dabbed at his eye.

Elgin, touched by the scene, cleared his throat and turned to one of the gun racks in embarrassment. Presently he broke the awkward silence:

"Er, Mr. Seven – no, I don't like the sound of that. Let me call you Will. Why don't you ride out to the ranch and see Betty? I know she'd like to see you again. Needless to say you made quite an impression on her. I think she'd be tickled if you came out. You know how girls are about heroes! Well, get settled and then come visit us. We'd love to have you, and oh – by the way" – he winked at Delevan and Will – "if Delevan doesn't have a job that suits you, stop in and see me. I may have something."

He said goodbye and left them staring at one another.

17.
Blank Paper

Delevan beamed at Will and hustled to the door, where he hung a "closed" sign in the window and locked the door. He drew the shades at the windows, and the three men retired to the back of the store where there were living quarters.

"Did you mean it?" asked Will, staring at Delevan.

"Did he mean what?" asked Storker.

"About the horse, about Black Boy! Is he mine?"

"Listen, Will," said Storker, answering for the smiling fat man, "if you got a certain piece of paper in your pocket, that horse is yours. In fact, we'll get you five horses just like that one. So much alike they'll be, that you can't tell them apart!"

"There could only be one horse like that one," said Will.

"Let me look at it," said Delevan. "Take it out and put it on the table here where I can read every word and figure on it. Get out the paper, Will. You got it, didn't you?"

Will nodded. "I got the paper all right."

"Well, get it out, son. What are you waitin' for? Let's look at it."

"There ain't nothin' on it," gulped Will, looking at them.

"There ain't nothin' on it," repeated Storker, growing white.

"Let me see it anyway," groaned Delevan.

Will took the folded piece of paper from his pocket and handed it to Delevan. The fat man received the bit of paper and began unfolding it, for it was folded many times into a small square. He said, "Nothing on it, eh, Will?"

"Just a couple of figures scribbled, that's all," murmured Will.

Delevan spread the paper flat on the table and smoothed it over with his heavy, fat hand. He sighed and breathed but one word: "Beautiful!"

"What's beautiful about it?" asked Storker. "Let me see it!" He snatched the paper away and held it so they could all see. "Why, it's nothing," he cried, "nothing but a code or something! It don't tell us nothing, Del, nothing at all! What's so beautiful about that?" He threw the paper back to the center of the table. It read:

N. 30°E. 115'

131

"It's a bearing," declared Delevan.

"A what?" asked Will and Cy as one.

"A bearing: that's a surveyor's term. It's a compass bearing; it means 30 degrees east of north," explained Delevan.

"What the hell good is that to us?" complained Cy. "What we need is a map, not a bearing."

"You fool!" said Del. "What good is any kind of map when you're working underground?"

"This is all we need, eh, Del?" asked Storker doubtfully.

"This is the thing that Dan Elgin tried to destroy," said Del, picking up the paper and staring fondly at it. "It's probably the only written record of this direction and distance. You see, Elgin paid a price to have this mark struck off the old map at Elwood, the county seat. I'll never forget that night." He sat back, looked at the others, and smiled.

"What night?" asked Will.

"The night Costain got this paper," answered Del. "It seems like it was only yesterday. But of course it was longer ago than I care to remember. Costain and I were just a couple of kids then – not much older than you, Will. We were working for old man Bogeman; that old rascal had picked us up out of the streets and was in the process of making

132

a couple of crooks out of us. We were doing mostly penny-ante stuff for the old geezer at that time, and after every job we'd go in and give him his split, which was 75 per cent of anything we got in our stick-ups. We had just started to get in on some of the big jobs that night when we were in Elwood."

He paused to light a cigar. He continued:

"Bogeman was gettin' set to knock off the express office in Elwood, and at that time they was both in the same building – the county records, I mean, and the express office. We were right outside the window. It was night. We could peek right in and see Elgin arguing with the county clerk. Dan was a lot younger then, and he was a handsome man in the soft glow of the lamp. The clerk was a little wizened-up fellow who had worked there for years. He was as straight as a bowstring, people said. Elgin was leaning over a map on the counter. 'What difference does it make if you erase one bearing on an old map like this?' says he. 'A lot of difference,' says the old-timer. 'Here's $1,000 in twenties,' says Dan. 'I'll just scratch the ink off with my pen-knife,' says the old-timer as he pocketed the stack of bills.

"Costain looks at me and I look at Cost, but we were both thinking one thing, and that was – What's on that map that can be worth a

133

thousand for one scratch with a knife? Then just as the fellow was starting to work with his penknife, Elgin yells: 'Just a minute! I'll just jot that down,' and he reached for a sheet of paper. Well, he jotted it down and was waving it in the air, waiting for the ink to dry, when a little gust of wind puffs through the office. You know how that can happen in the summertime?"

The listeners nodded.

Delevan continued: "That paper floated through the air like it was a swallow dipping along the ground, and it flew right out the window. Lee snapped out his fist to snatch it from me, for I was grabbing at it also. Elgin let out a yell and came running outside, but we ducked up the alley and hid under some old crates. I was a sight smaller in those days, and could dash about and do things like that. Elgin came out with the old man and they looked all around, but they couldn't find the paper, of course. Elgin took this to be a sort of omen, and he said: 'Well, this is a good lesson. Perhaps I should forget about recording it; even if somebody found the paper it would mean nothing to anyone else.' He went back inside and we took off with the paper. Of course, we never said a word to old Bogeman about the paper. Long Lee slung it around his neck in that pouch,

134

and there it's been till this day. All Lee knows about that paper is that it's worth a thousand to Dan Elgin."

He paused, winded at the length of his narrative.

"How is this bearing, as you call it, going to help us to Elgin's $600,000?" asked Will.

"That's easy," said Delevan.

"It means a hell of a lot less mucking," murmured Cy, and then he added, looking at his hands, "I hope."

"Mucking?" said Will, perplexed.

"Listen, Will, you know anything about the history of this town?" asked Delevan.

"No."

"Well, all this country around here used to belong to the Mexicans. There was a regular settlement of them here. This used to be the very center of things; in fact, it was right about here that the main plaza was located. You know how the Spanish are about their plazas?"

"They like a good spacious plaza," declared Will.

"That's right," said Del. "Now, what's the name of this town?"

"Three Wells, of course," said Will.

The fat man smiled. "And how many wells do you see out there? In the street, I mean."

"Why, one is all."

135

"That's right – one well, near the horse trough. Now, what do you know about Elgin's bank?" asked the bank robber.

"Only that the actual vault is set in an old well, carved of solid rock with a steel cover and a heavy combination, and that the cellar of the bank is a maze of passages, a regular puzzle, they say. Nobody ever robbed it yet. I guess it's about the safest bank along this part of the range. Outside of that, I don't know much about the bank," said Will.

"That's as much as most know," said Del, and he added, "and a bit more. Now, the bearing on this piece of paper is going to take us right into that bank – with your help!"

"How can I help now?"

"Get out to the Elgin Ranch and play up to that girl all you can. Find out where the bench mark is."

"What's a bench mark?" asked Will.

"A bench mark is a surveyor's mark from which other things are located. The bank vault is thirty degrees east of north if you were standing right over the bench mark. If we can find the bench mark we can lay this thing out and dig our way right into the bottom of Dan's vault. We can get our own bearings from the bench mark – that's easy – and then we can lay the whole thing out on paper. Where the two lines intersect – that's

136

the direction we dig in from now on. We've already started to dig, of course, on a pure guess on our part; but now we can correct ourselves and dig straight as a shaft of light for the third well!"

"Where's the second one?" gasped Will, for the complexity of these plans amazed him.

"You're sitting on it, my boy," said Delevan, smiling.

Will looked down at the floor.

Delevan added: "You see, this was all part of the old plaza. When the Americans drove the Mexicans out of here, they latched on to the plaza as the most desirable real estate. Of course, two of the wells were dry. So they built right over those. Sheldon built his store over one and Elgin his bank over the other."

"Why don't you get over to the county seat at Elwood and find out this bench mark, or whatever you call it, from the Records Office?" asked Will, suspiciously.

"The old records were all destroyed by fire," declared Delevan. "Everything back past seventy is gone. Elgin is probably the only man alive who knows where it is. You've got to pry it out of him or his daughter – somehow."

137

18.
Drill, Shoot, and Muck!

"I don't like it," declared Seven.

"How do you like the sound of $200,000?" asked Storker with a crooked grin.

"I don't mind the thought of that," murmured Will. "I might be able to get around the girl and the old man. But can you do all these other things? Can you take a piece of paper and figure out how these lines and bearings and everything that you're talking about will intersect?"

"Del can," said Storker proudly.

"Well, can you tunnel into that other well? I mean, doesn't that take a lot of skill?" Will asked.

"Cy is the answer to that," said Delevan. "He's been boring ahead for days now. The cellar is partly filled with rock already. Isn't it, Cy?"

"Sure," said the thin man proudly. "All there is to tunneling in rock is to drill, shoot, and muck, and then drill, shoot, and muck again."

"Mucking? That's what you said before,"

said Will "What is this mucking?"

Storker grinned. "Well, kid, first you *drill* a hole, see. Then you fill it with blasting powder; *shoot* it off; then you *muck* out the loose stone. Drill – shoot – muck: they're just terms used by tunnelers, that's all," explained Storker.

"It seems like all I'm learnin' lately is new terms," murmured Will, looking around at them. "How in the hell can you two blast – underground though it is – without somebody hearing you?"

They both started to laugh as though he had made the greatest of jokes. Delevan rocked gently back and forth in his chair, laughter pouring from his body, and Storker kept slapping his thigh as he roared; but eventually even this wasn't enough of an outlet for him, and he rose and rocked about the room, laughing and gasping for breath. Delevan continued to laugh until the tears rolled down his fat cheeks. Presently he gasped out:

"It's easy, Will; especially when you shoot off your blast at exactly the same time every day! You see, people get to expect it and they don't think anything of it."

"How can that be?" asked Will, staring incredulously at them.

"Oh, boy," gasped Cy, "you tell him, Del; it's too much for me – you tell him."

"You see, Will," began Delevan, "we've got this big cannon outside – you probably saw it as you rode up. We shoot it off every noon. It's a time signal – so we tell folks! They eat it up. They think it's a great idea. Ha, ha, ho – ah, ho, ho – they don't know that every noon takes us five feet closer to their money!"

"But I don't see . . . Wait a minute! You mean that both blasts go off at the same time?" asked Will, his face lighting up, as he began to see the deviltry of the scheme.

"That's it!" admitted Storker.

"By golly, that's a dandy stunt," said Will, laughing with them.

Delevan had dried his eyes, and was calmer now as he explained more of the details.

"We can drill the holes any time because that doesn't make much noise, you see. But the blast, that's a different tune. We have to time the blast to go at twelve o'clock, right along with the cannon. Oh, I can tell you that the cannon has surprised a lot of folks with the vibration it sets up!" He laughed again, winking at Will.

"It's foolproof," said Cy. "Why, even Elgin was down in his vault one day at noon. And he comes out after the cannon had fired, and whatta you think he says?"

"What did he say?" asked Will, grinning.

"He says – oh, haw, haw," gasped Storker, carried away by the memory – "He says, 'You know, Cy, that cannon shakes my vault some!' That's what he said," howled the gaunt Storker, delighted to tears.

Will turned to Delevan. "How did you get the town to swallow this cannon going off all the time?"

"That was easy; we told them that it was a time signal. You see, every noon we shoot the damn cannon, and pretty soon people start to set their watches by it. People are like animals, Will; just get them used to some noise, and first thing you know they don't hear it any more."

"That's good," said Will. "I'll remember that. Can I go down and look at the digging – I mean mucking!"

They laughed.

Storker glanced at Delevan for approval, and upon seeing an almost imperceptible nod of the ponderous head he quickly snatched one of the battered rugs aside, revealing a trap door. This was the conventional means of entering a cellar in that locality. Delevan squeaked up the globe of a rusty lantern and held it near the hole as Storker and Seven went down the ladder. Will descended into the dank, wet-smelling cellar.

A heavy coating of dust lay everywhere –

evidence of the blasting that had taken place. A great portion of the cellar was already filled with rock that Storker had taken out. Will could see, as Delevan came down the ladder, its old rungs creaking and straining under each transfer of his bulk, that the walls of the old stone-lined well were still intact. He noticed that the partial cellar of the old Sheldon place had been dug right around the old well, the top stones of which had been knocked off to make room for the beams of the floor.

A large hole had been battered in the side of the well casing. Delevan walked to the opening and leaned in, holding the lantern so that the interior was well lighted.

Will was surprised that the tunnel had advanced so far, for while all he could see of it was a gaping hole with a portion of the beginning lighted, he could also perceive that enough rock had been removed to fill the bottom of the well and part of the cellar besides.

"How far have you gone?" asked Will of Storker.

"About thirty feet." Cy smiled. "But we gotta correct the direction soon; you can see that we're running into some sand here and there, and we're sure that the other well is cut in solid rock. Of course, we're angling down, too, so as to hit Elgin's well below ground!" It was clear that Cy was exceedingly proud of the work he had done.

"Let's go upstairs," said Delevan, shivering in the dank atmosphere. "We can go out and have a good meal. No use digging any further till we find out where the bench mark is."

They climbed the ladder and closed the door to the cellar behind them. They went across the street to the hotel, where Delevan ordered for them all, and Will wondered why Cy did not grow fat on Delevan's menus. They lounged on the porch of the store after supper until Storker rose and said:

"I'm for the hay. I need the sleep. There's a bunk back there for you, kid." He nodded at Will.

"Thanks," said Will, "only don't call me 'kid'!"

Storker disappeared without argument.

Delevan shifted his cigar and smoked a while before he broke the silence by saying:

"Perhaps you'd better ride out to the Elgin ranch tomorrow, while the invitation is still fresh. See the girl, chat a while, and try to make some impression upon them. Watch your language out there. You're a good kid, see; the breaks have all been against you. Act humble, talk soft. Be polite, use words like 'sir' and 'ma'am.' Lay it on thick. If

Elgin offers you a job, feign loyalty to me but let him win you over. Don't get in any fights with that crew of his. I dare say they'll let you alone in any case. Can you remember all that?"

"Maybe if I wrote it down." Will laughed.

"You'll remember – you scamp," murmured Delevan around his cigar. The fat man rose heavily from his chair and left the porch for his sleeping quarters.

Will rolled a cigarette and smiled into the darkness. In his life of ups and downs he had thirsted for revenge on those who had hounded him, and Dan Elgin was a symbol of them all. He looked forward to hurting the high-and-mighty Elgin. The plan looked foolproof to him.

19.
In the Hay

Will awoke early and made his preparations for the trip out to the Elgin Ranch. This consisted mainly of washing and grooming himself as carefully as possible and cleaning as much of the dust from his clothes as time allowed. He was equally fastidious in the preparation of the black stallion. Delevan awoke briefly before he left and bombarded him with last-minute advice on the treatment of the girl, the right things to say to Dan Elgin, what not to say and do, and other things that he thought might help. Then the fat man promptly fell back asleep with a satisfied grin.

The town was quiet as Will walked the short distance to the livery stable; this was not strange, for it was Sunday morning. There was no church in Three Wells, but he could hear the church bell ringing plainly from Rebel Hill, the neighboring town. He thought that Sunday was a funny day to call on the Elgins, but he reasoned that he could explain that away by saying he would have to work during the week. Actually, he had always avoided work. While he had watched many another engaged in some occupation, he had managed somehow always to elude the habit himself.

He followed the directions of Delevan and soon found himself within sight of the Elgin Ranch. The beauty of it took him aback. He knew that Elgin was rich, and he had expected an unusually fine home, but its grandeur was more than he had thought it would be.

145

The barn, of course, stood out as the largest building from a distance. It was a huge structure with a gigantic gambrel roof standing up above everything else. Inside, he knew, would be a great loft capable of storing tons of hay. The storage of a great deal of hay could only mean one thing: the ranch was rich in horses; evidence of this he could see as he passed a large herd of mares. It seemed that at least two dozen colts were frolicking about in the pasture.

A magnificent stallion stood watching from a fenced-off section of the lot. He called to the horse, but it paid no attention to the rider and black stallion.

Will looked ahead at the ranch. A long, low bunkhouse stood to one side, and there were several smaller barns, one of which appeared to be used as a stable. Around all these buildings was a good deal of grass, as well as tall shade trees. It was a beautiful sight, and he envied Dan and Mary Elgin.

The house was of frame construction, two stories tall with a long rambling porch that ran completely around the outside of it. A picket fence closed the yard against intrusion by horse or rider. All the buildings were bright with fresh paint, but for all its prosperity the place seemed to be deserted. No one stirred near the bunkhouse or main house. The doors of the barn were closed.

Will dismounted before the fence and tied the stallion to a hitch rack under a large horse-chestnut tree. He looked around. The absence of human movement made him self-conscious as he lifted the gate latch and walked up the narrow gravel path to the front door, and knocked.

There was no answer. He knocked again. Though he heard light footsteps coming downstairs, no one answered the door. A slight movement to one side caught his eye, and he turned to see a curtain shift back into position. A girl's voice called, "Just a moment."

Next he heard the girl running back upstairs. Five minutes passed before Will, staring at the door in an embarrassed manner, turned to leave the porch.

"Here I am," cried a voice behind him.

Will turned, and took off his hat. "Hello," he said.

She was, he found, not so plump as he had thought her. She was clothed simply in a blue silk dress with short sleeves. He noted that while the neckline was very womanly, revealing her well-rounded figure, the length of the dress was more girlish, and ended midway between her ankles and knees.

While he had had a fairly clear picture

of her in his mind, he was not altogether prepared for her smooth brown skin and jet-black hair. Though Will had never been bashful, now, face to face with the girl as he was, everything seemed to fail him, and apart from his greeting he could think of nothing to say or do.

Mary's dancing black eyes froze his tongue and made his heart beat so wildly that he dared not risk conversation. The scent of lavender was carried to him on the breeze. Almost panicky, he retreated to the porch railing.

She smiled. "Well?" she asked.

"Hello."

"You said that."

"I did?"

"Of course you did. Daddy told me you were goin' to ride out and see us. I'm glad you did. Is it true, all the things they say about you?"

"What things?" he asked defensively.

"That you're poison to train robbers, that you can ride like the wind, and that you're a crack shot?"

"Why, that's mostly exaggeration," said Will with a smile.

"Will you stay to dinner?" she invited, eyeing him boldly.

"Well, that would be up to your father, I

148

suppose. You remember he had his crew work me over pretty good just for grinnin' a little at you that day."

She frowned. "You were wonderful. Where did you learn to fight like that?"

"All around," he replied, with a shrug.

"Would you like to come in and see the house?" she asked.

He looked at her and then over his shoulder.

"Where is everybody?" he asked.

"All the hands are in Rebel Hill, attendin' church. Daddy is out lookin' over his herd. He's way out; he'll be gone a while. Don't worry."

"Whatta you mean, don't worry?" he gasped.

"You're afraid to come in with me, aren't you?"

"Why, of course not; only, it seems funny – I mean, all your hands goin' to church. Don't you ever go to church?"

"Oh, that. There's a new widow over in Rebel Hill who's got every man on the range chasin' her. Humph. Well, I'm not goin' over there and watch all the boys make fools of themselves. Yes, I used to go to church all the time."

Will smiled and said, "She must be some looker, eh?"

149

"She ain't much," declared Mary. "Too big around here." She passed her hand across her chest in a little gesture.

"Come on in, Will," she said. "I won't bite you."

Will followed her into the house. She took him first to the kitchen, and he remarked about the big black, shiny stove.

"The parlor is this way," she murmured, and brushed by him in the doorway as she went through.

The contact startled him. She whirled about and stood with her face inches away. He leaned back, amazed at her closeness.

"What's the matter?" she purred.

"It's hot in here," he gasped.

"Step over here in the parlor," she urged. "We have a real cool parlor!"

She took his hand in both of hers and tugged at him. The smooth softness of her hands thrilled him and made him swallow hard. His heart started beating wildly again. He let her pull him into the parlor. Carefully he seated himself on the settee.

She sat down tight against him. He looked painfully at all the empty space. She continued to hold his hand. He glanced quickly at her and away again, for he found that she was gazing fondly at him. Suddenly she started to give his hand a series of little squeezes.

"Holy cow!" he said, running his fingers around his collar.

"What?" she sighed, as though she hadn't heard him.

"I said, let's step out in the sun, where it's cooler."

"Would you like to look around outside?"

"That would be better."

They went to the door hand in hand.

She took him on a tour of the buildings. He found that he was applying pressure now, to the grip of her hand. They paused before the great barn.

"This is some whopper of a barn," Will said, looking up.

"It holds a pile of hay," she admitted. "Come on in."

"Oh, I couldn't; I mean, we better not," Will cautioned.

"Why not?"

"Well –"

"You wouldn't harm me, would you?" she asked, smiling up at him.

"Of course not." He scowled.

"Then let's go in and look it over," she said, sliding the big door back.

They stepped inside.

"Shut the door," she advised. "There are windows."

He closed the door, shutting out the bright

151

shaft of sunlight, and found that the few windows dimly lighted the barn, as she had said. They were standing in a small section of the main floor that was devoted to stalls for the work-horses. They passed by six gigantic percherons that were stamping their feet and switching their tails. The horses were pulling at the hay in the bins before them. At the end of the stalls they came to a narrow stair.

"Wait until you see this mow," she promised, and led the way.

They came out of the stairway and into the upper part of the barn. Will whistled softly at the great size of the structure.

"You could hold some dance up here!" he exclaimed.

"We have." She smiled. "Do you like to dance? Hold me and dance a little." She hummed a little tune, coming closer to him.

"What –" He started to speak, but found that he was holding her and indeed dancing with her.

They whirled about the cleared space on the floor as she half hummed and half sang a waltz tune.

They stopped suddenly, and she raised up on her toes and kissed him. He staggered back, pulling at her arms, which were firmly clasped around his neck. She kissed him again and again. He stopped struggling and stood

152

still, kissing her back. Presently they both stopped and, panting, stared at each other. He smiled at her. She took his hand and led him to the loose hay near the spot the mangers were fed from. She collapsed into the fragrant hay and pulled him with her.

"We better get out of here," said Will, listening for other sounds.

"Nobody'll be back for a while," she purred. "Kiss me some more. You kiss awful nice. Where'd you learn to kiss like that? What kind of kissin' do you call that?"

"Nuthin' – it's just regular kissing," he gasped, bending over her once more.

"Rub my ears some more," she pleaded. "Here, hold still; let me kiss you. . . . Do you like that? Gosh, your hair is soft; you have awful soft hair for a boy, don't you? Squeeze me a little."

"Listen, Mary, I'll get tarred and feathered if your old – I mean, if your father finds us. We'd better get out of here."

"Kiss me a little more, Will, *please?*"

"All right, just a little bit, Mary; then we gotta get out of this hay."

"That's it; kiss me like that – oh, the muscles in your arms are just like steel cords, and your back is all covered with muscle too." She sighed.

"Your hair is gettin' all moist and wispy,

like," he murmured, brushing some strands from her eyes.

"I love you, Will Seven."

"Mary, you're wonderful." Will choked, looking down at her.

"Kiss my eyes closed," she sighed.

A whoop in the distance preceded the sound of an approaching band of horsemen. Will sat up suddenly and stared at the girl.

"Oh, migosh! The boys are comin' back! Quick! down the stairs and out the back way," she gasped.

They ran for the stairs.

20.
On the Porch

Mary flew before him, scarcely touching the stairs as they descended. Will ran cursing behind her, trying to keep pace by taking the stairs two at a time. The low beams made this hazardous, however. It would not be wise, he felt, to appear before Dan Elgin with a fresh lump or gash on his head. He snatched frantically at the cobwebs that he gathered in the hasty flight, trying to clear them away.

Mary dashed past the row of work horses and slid open the rear door just as they heard the riders reining up and dismounting at the front of the barn. She leaned back as Will came up to her on the run. She kissed him again quickly, then led the way out into the back field. They had run to a point in the field at least a hundred feet from the back of the barn. She took his hand and led him strolling casually farther into the field and angling toward the house. As they reached a point that would bring them within sight of the cowboys, she squeezed his hand and turned toward the house. They thus came into the sight of the others, looking as if they were just returning from a stroll in the field.

Will noticed the glances the cowboys were directing toward him, and he looked at the girl's clothing and his own to make sure all traces of the barn were gone. He brushed some cobwebs from his shirt; Mary looked fresh and cool. He saw the black-bearded foreman, Chuck Mace, swagger belligerently toward them.

"Here it comes," groaned Will, out of the side of his mouth.

"Here what comes?" she said.

"Here's where I pay for those kisses in the barn."

She smiled up at him.

155

"Weren't they worth it?" she teased.

"That depends on how much Chuck and his friends charge," murmured Will, glancing toward the approaching cowboy. The other hands held their distance as Will and Mary neared the fence around the house.

Mace said: "What's this tramp doin' here, Miss Mary? Does Mr. Elgin know he's out here?"

She flounced her dark hair in anger as she turned toward the foreman. She said: "Daddy invited Mr. Seven out here. He's *not* a tramp. You may leave us be!"

"Yeah, well, maybe he's not a tramp. Maybe he's a crook, though. I don't believe all of that train-robber-hero stuff!"

"Maybe you'd better shut up, dirty face," snarled Will.

Mace stiffened. "Dirty face!" he gasped. "Why, you little son —"

"Oh, go water your horse or I'll knock your teeth down your throat. Go on. Get out of here and leave Mary and me alone or else you'll be damn sorry," said Will, laughing a little at the expression of the other.

"Here comes Daddy in his rig now," cried the girl, breaking the tension.

Mace turned to stare at the approaching buggy. "You're lucky, Seven; this is your lucky day, all right. Next time I see you

156

alone I'm gonna beat the hell out of you. I'm gonna smash yore nose and crunch out all your teeth, damn you. I hate you, Seven, and I'm gonna kill you if I get the chance, see?"

"Mr. Mace," shrilled the girl, going up on her tiptoes. "Mr. Seven is a guest in my father's house – is that clear?"

Mace glared at the girl, then stared out into the fields at the approaching rig. He wheeled back toward them and stepped toward Will with a growl. He checked himself, however, giving them both a look of profound disgust, and turned back toward the other cowboys.

Will, who had tensed for a sudden struggle, breathed a sigh of relief that the conversation between himself, Mace, and the girl had been at a tone that was not heard by the other hands. For had Mace received the tongue lashing within earshot of the cowboys, he could never have backed down and maintained his authority at the ranch. Mace was willing enough, however, under the circumstances, to let the matter drop rather than risk a falling out with the owner, who was rapidly approaching.

Will passed through the gate with Mary and stood on the porch as Dan Elgin wheeled his smart team past them at a brisk clip and skidded the buggy to a stop not far from the circle of cowhands. Mace was instantly up

157

to the owner of the ranch, gesticulating and talking and pointing toward the house. Elgin turned and, perceiving the young people, waved a friendly greeting toward them. They waved back.

Elgin said something, and Mace slumped off, leading his horse. The rest of the hands followed, except for two who took care of the team for Elgin.

On the porch, Mary said, "You wait here and talk to Daddy, Honey, I've got to start dinner."

"Don't call me Honey!" said Will.

"Sweetie?" she cooed.

"Listen," choked Will, regarding the approaching banker, "I mean – in front of your father – er – don't say anything that will make him think we –"

"All right." She smiled. "I won't tell him you kissed me in the barn – yet!" She turned and hurried into the house.

Will sank into one of the chairs with a moan. The girl was making things very difficult, or so he thought. What if, with her mush love-making, she should ruin all the work that had been done so far? The struggle with Costain and Fred Strate, he thought, was hardly worth a mere marriage with Dan Elgin's daughter. Still, he found that he was rather fond of her. He had been

158

surprised at her strength in the barn.

Appearing tanned and alert, Elgin came up the porch steps and extended his hand. He was a vital, pleasant-appearing man when he dressed in clothes such as he now wore, Will decided.

"Sit down, sit down. Make yourself at home," invited Elgin, as Will rose to meet him.

"Thanks," said Will, dropping into the chair once more.

"Didn't I see Mary out here a minute ago?" asked Elgin, taking the chair near Will.

"She's inside, getting dinner," said Will; then he added, "She asked me to stay, but I suppose I should be getting back."

"Why, what's the hurry?"

"Well, Delevan has some things he wants to show me about the store – you know how Del is."

"An odd chap, that one," murmured Elgin.

"He's been good to me," defended Will.

"Right. Right you are. And that's what counts – how you're treated I mean. That's why you're having dinner with us today. Delevan isn't going to work you on Sunday, anyway. Let Delevan work on Sunday if he wants to, but you and I – well, we'll just sit back and take it easy. As a matter of fact, I think we ought to make this a regular Sunday

159

practice – having you out here to dinner, I mean. What do you think of that?"

Will smiled. "Well, I guess I can stay – just for this time, though."

"Wonderful! Mary. Oh, Mary. Set an extra plate, please. Will is staying for dinner with us," he called over his shoulder.

"I already have," came the reply.

Elgin shifted around in his chair. It was obvious to Will that the other was eager to discuss something with him; he presumed that it was the $20,000 reward money.

"Say, I've got a jug in the house. What do you say we have a cup while we're waiting for dinner?" asked Elgin.

"I could drink a cup," said Will.

21.
In the Cup

Elgin tiptoed from the porch, making a wry face and holding his finger to his lips, indicating, it seemed, that Will was not to say anything that would alert the girl inside as to the mission of the banker.

Will heard several doors close and a step

on some stairs, then all was quiet. Presently Elgin reappeared, burdened by a huge stone jug and two cups. It was evident that the jug had been stored in a cool place, for already the outer surface was dimpled with moisture.

Elgin seated himself and poured a liberal portion for Will and a half-cup for himself. He sat down, the jug beside him.

Will smiled to himself as the banker looked away, for the game of the other was obvious to him.

"Here's to money," toasted Elgin, raising his glass; "you can't live without it."

Will smiled and drained his glass. His eyes watered suddenly as the powerful whisky hit home. He fought to maintain his composure under the sharp eye of Elgin, who had gaped at his quickly swallowed cup and was now scrutinizing Will for some sign of the effect; the banker ignored his own drink.

"Aren't you going to finish it?" asked Will, eyeing his host's drink.

"What? Oh. Why, yes, bottoms up! Oh, God – that *has* got a belt, eh? Makes me shudder a little to drain a glass like that." His whole body convulsed from the draught of whisky. He looked at Will and said: "How about another? Good! I thought you would. Here, let me pour it."

As he bent to the task of pouring from the

heavy jug, Will could see that he again gave himself a half-portion.

"What will your duties be if you go to work for Delevan? I mean what can you do?" pried Elgin.

"Why, anything Del wants, I suppose. There's few things I can't do," admitted the other matter-of-factly.

"Well, I like a man with confidence in himself," murmured Elgin, "but you don't look like a man who knows any trade."

"I'm a jack-of-all-trades," said Will with a smile.

"Master of none, eh!" retorted Elgin.

"Master of some, perfectionist at others. I've worked at them all. They bore me for the most part. I like excitement," commented Will.

Elgin appeared interested after this last admission, and he started to say, "Well, just give me –"

"The brown mare has a stone under her shoe," interrupted Will, pointing toward one of the horses in the pasture.

"What? Where?" asked Elgin, sitting forward and straining his eyes.

With a flick of his wrist Will dumped his cup of whisky over the side of the porch and into the bushes.,

Elgin turned back. "By golly, she does at

162

that. You've got a sharp eye, Seven! What? Cup empty again. Well, if you're gonna drink with a man, be a man and drink equal, I always say." He drained his cup.

"Ugh." He grimaced. "Strong stuff, eh?"

"Tastes good; not much body, though," shrugged Will with a smile.

"What!" exclaimed Elgin. "Here, have another. That's the first time anybody ever said my stuff didn't have body. By fortune, you'll feel some body when you drink your third cup." He poured.

Will accepted it.

"What were you gonna ask me," asked Will, "before I interrupted you?"

"I was going to ask what trades you'd worked at in your travels. What are some of the jobs you've held? Say there's a cobweb on your shoulder there. There, I've got it off for you."

"Thanks," said Will, glancing at the bit of cobweb. "Well, I've been a mason, for one thing."

"That must be a boring job," said Elgin dryly.

"I never got any of the boring ones," smiled Will. "You must mean standing still and laying bricks or stones all day or something like that, eh? No, they always gave me the hard stuff to do. Did you ever see the arch

163

over the main entrance to the Chase Bank in New York?"

"You worked on that?" gasped Elgin.

"Twenty-four stones – each weighing almost a ton apiece." Will smiled. "Took me three days; of course, I had six good masons working with me. On the third day I had them lower the keystone into place, and it fit like it was chiseled for the hole on the spot instead of in a stone quarry a thousand miles away. My boss made some money on that job." He continued: "Of course, that type of work is nothing like the botch job on your well over there."

It was clear that the well was a prideful thing to Dan Elgin, for it was a pleasingly constructed object. Elgin whirled about to stare at his own well, hardly able to believe that someone could speak derisively about it. As he turned, Will again dumped his glass and raised the empty cup to his lips, letting the drop or two that remained trickle down his chin.

Elgin smiled at the empty cup as he turned back.

"Let's have another before dinner," he said, slurring his words slightly. He poured the cups, smiling all the while at his trickery. He added: "Well, there may be a little too much mortar on the joints or something like

164

that, but our well is a good piece of mason work for around here."

"It's like everything out here in the West," said Will: "sloppy. Why, just look at that cornice over your door."

"What's wrong with that?" asked Elgin, turning and leaning forward in his chair as he did so.

Will used the moment to pour most of his cup into Elgin's, who by this time was rather bleary-eyed and uncertain of his movements. Will drained the rest of his cup before answering.

"I've seen a thousand cornices that were layed out and cut better than that. Look at the poor work on the miters there!"

"By gawd, I never noticed it before this," said Elgin, staring hard to see Will at all.

"Let me fill you up while I pour myself another," said Will, getting the jug. "This stuff does seem to have a little body at that."

"You're right ish got body," commented Elgin; "but wait till I dri –" he hiccuped – "drink this. You're gettin' ahead." He drained it.

Will poured more whisky.

"How come you came West?" asked Elgin, fighting to pronounce his words clearly. He blinked his eyes several times. "You should have been a great success back East."

165

"I worked my way out here running lines," said Will.

"What? Whash lines?"

"Surveying. Running lines. Surveying land and such," said Will. His heart leaped, for in actuality he knew very little about the profession of land surveying, and what little he did know had been gleaned from occasionally watching some surveyor. He knew scarcely a dozen terms familiar to the field. He greatly feared that he would say something that even Elgin, in his present drunken condition, would detect as being not true.

"You're surveyor too? Shay, you do know a lot!" blurted Elgin looking into his own empty cup and thirstily pouring himself another. "How'd you like to do surveys for the bank? With my legal training and you doing the surveying, we could make some sharp land deals. You in'rested anything like that?"

"No," said Will. "What good is a surveyor in a God-forsaken hole like Three Wells? Why, stop and think for minute. What's the first thing a surveyor needs?"

"Tools, I shuppose," slurred Elgin, sagging to the side in his chair. His arm was extended and the contents of his cup were spilling on to the porch floor.

"Instruments, yes, but more important

166

than that, Elgin – a bench mark! Why, I'll wager there isn't a bench mark within a thousand miles of Three Wells. No, Mr. Elgin, it'll be a good many years before they run lines this far and establish a bench mark!"

"Thash no prob – problem," said Elgin, his eyes closing slightly; "there's one right on the rim of the town well!"

Will leaped up from the chair, the sweat standing out on his brow, so great was the importance of Elgin's remark. Elgin greeted his movement with a snore, having fallen asleep for the time being.

"Dinner's ready!" called Mary, from inside the doorway.

Will wiped his brow. "Mary! Oh, Mary, would you step out here for a minute?" he called.

He heard her step in the hallway. "What's the matter Will?" she asked sweetly as she came through the door. "Oh, migosh – Dad! Drinking again, eh! Well that finishes that old jug, by gosh. I'll empty it into the garden."

"Better wait until tomorrow," advised Will, glancing over the rail at the moist ground.

"All right, Will," she said, her voice resigned, "you get him under the arms and I'll take his feet."

They carried the banker into the house and managed to get him to his bed. Will pulled off his boots, and as they stepped back, panting, Elgin passed into a deep sleep. They tiptoed out and closed the door.

"You'll still stay for dinner just the same, won't you, Will?" asked the girl, looking up at him.

"Of course," he said, putting his arm around her waist.

22.
Delevan Gives Odds

Will left the Elgin ranch within two hours of the time he and Mary had finished eating. He had several reasons for doing so. He didn't want to be there when Elgin awoke, and he didn't want to be traveling the trail back to Three Wells near dark with feeling between himself and Chuck Mace being what it was. Also, he was eager to speak with Delevan and inform the outlaw of the location of the bench mark. Neither was he anxious to spend too much time with the girl, for while he enjoyed her passion he was afraid that the hands would think something amiss if he overstayed and they did not see or hear

168

anything of the banker for such a long time.

In spite of the fact that he thought he had ridden away from the ranch without a great deal of surveillance from the hands, he still stopped frequently to watch his back trail. During one of these pauses he led his horse from the trail and into a jumble of rocks. He hobbled the stallion and climbed up high among the rocks to gaze along the trail behind him. He was rewarded for his vigilance when he descried Chuck Mace and two others furiously urging their mounts along the road.

He returned to the horse and, clamping his hand on the muzzle of the animal, waited, watching from covert as Mace and the others swept around the bend. They drew up in the spot where Will had left the trail, cursing and hollering as they looked down the long sloping road that led from that spot right into Three Wells. The ground fell away at a gentle pitch for miles from that point, and it was clear to them that their quarry had already reached the town.

"That damn stallion must have flown," exclaimed Chuck.

Another of the riders cursed. "I'll be lame for a week, Chuck. I tried to tell you he had too much start and too much horse for any of our nags."

"If I hadda taken the old man's mare we'd

'a' caught him," groaned Mace.

"Say," said the third man, "do yuh suppose the old man really was sleepin' like Mary said?"

"Seems funny. I'd be damned if I'd go to sleep and leave my daughter with a stranger," said one of the cowboys, turning his horse around. "How about you, Chuck?"

"To hell with it all," swore Mace, spurring off back to the ranch and leaving the other two.

The two cowboys looked at each other and galloped after him.

Will smiled and led the stallion down from the rocks. He mounted up again and headed the horse toward town at an easy lope. He was amazed at the success he had in getting the secret from Elgin, although he realized that the bench mark meant little without the bearing that was in Delevan's possession. He frowned when he thought of Mary. Her wild kisses were troubling his conscience. He did not dwell on the thought of hurting her through the robbery of her father's bank.

It was dusk when he arrived back in Three Wells; he didn't go directly to the store, but left his horse at the livery stable first. Will disdained letting the operator of the establishment take care of the stallion, however, preferring to tend to the horse

170

himself. After Black Boy had been carefully dried and grained, Will wandered up the main street and approached the store softly, whistling a tune. Delevan and Storker were seated on the porch during the early evening hours, as was their custom.

They had been careful to remain within sight of the inhabitants of the town as much as possible. After dark they did some of the digging, and while one of them was tending the store the other would occasionally muck out some of the loose stone. Of course, the drilling had to be done every day and the charge set to time the blast with the noise of the cannon.

It was their usual practice to rest during those hours when the heat of the day was abating and the coolness of the night coming on. On occasion they spent time in the saloon across the street, but tonight they had reason to sit on the porch, momentarily expecting the return of Seven. In many ways they were more excited about his return from this simple visit to the Elgin ranch than they were while awaiting his return from Lee Costain.

Noting his approach, Delevan said: "Look at him, Cy. Look at him swagger along. Oh, for the confidence of youth, eh? Listen – he's whistling, too."

Storker spat. "So he's whistling. What

does that prove? Does that prove he found anything? I tell you, Del, that kid doesn't give a tinker's dam about this whole deal. Why, he'd come walkin' in here whistlin' like that even if he'd never gone out there today. For that matter, maybe he *didn't go* out there. Did you ever think of that? He must be a liar. He lied his way into Costain's gang, didn't he?"

"Well, Cy, if that's any proof of anything, I recall hearing you do a little lying now and then." Delevan smiled, looking at the other.

"What the hell do you mean by that – you callin' me a liar, Del?"

"Don't be so thin-skinned, Cy. What I'm trying to say is that a crook has to be a liar of necessity, and the better liar he is, the better crook he'll be."

"You and your sayings," growled Cy as Will stepped up onto the porch.

"Back early, eh, Will?" greeted Storker.

"Yeah, I didn't want to come back in the dark. Those hands of Elgin's don't think too much of me. Even so, they tried to catch me on the way back."

"Is that so?" asked Cy, his voice tinged with doubt and suspicion.

Will looked at him. "What's the matter with him?" he asked, nodding his head toward Storker.

172

"He's just a little tired of digging, I guess," said Del.

"Well, he can stop talking like that to me or he'll have somebody digging for him – six by six," said Will.

"Stop this damn bickering," cursed Delevan. "You know what we want to hear. Did you make progress? Did you find out anything? How did you hit it off with the girl?"

"I knocked her for a loop," smiled Will. "She's nuts about me, it seems. She sure kissed up a storm when I was up in Elgin's hayloft with her!"

"By Gawd, now I know he's lying in his teeth," said Storker, almost jealously.

"*I* believe him," admonished Del. "What else happened?"

"I had a little brush with Mace, but nothing come of it. He threatened to get me –"

"Never mind that," interrupted Delevan. "We'll take care of Mace if he comes around. He'll wish he'd stayed out on the range with the steers. How about Elgin? Did he try to hire you or anything? That's what I had him figured to do."

"He didn't get around to offering me a job," declared Will.

"Why not?" asked Delevan, sitting up, his tone of voice disappointed.

173

"Well, he was too busy talking about other things, I guess." Will smiled, enjoying the agony of suspense he was creating.

Delevan jumped up, his fat face radiant with expectation.

"You got it, didn't you? By God, Cy, Will got it! I'll lay fifty-to-one odds on it. I can see it dancing in his eyes, I can see it there waiting to be let out. You're playing with us, eh, Will?"

Storker reached into his pocket to pull forth a fat wallet. He sneered at Will and said, "I'll just take $100 worth of those odds!" He peeled a large bill off the stack.

"You're covered," panted Delevan, his small eyes glistening in the darkness.

He added: "Come, come, Will; who wins?"

"You do. The bench mark is on the rim of the well – right over there in the street."

"Whoopee!" screamed Delevan, forgetting his usual composure and rushing across the porch to Storker. He plucked the thin crook from his chair as if he were a sack of onions and began dancing around the floor in a merry whirl. Will marveled at the huge man's grace.

"Put me down, you damn fool!" shouted Storker. "I wanta see that mark before I pay!"

"Come on then, Cy; you're gonna see it." Laughing, Delevan hurried the other toward the well in the street.

To cover their actions Will dropped the bucket splashing into the depths and began, after allowing time for the weighted vessel to sink, to wind up the winch.

As Delevan moved slowly around the rim, he murmured: "I've been around here fifty times, but I've never noticed anything. Still, what you're not looking for –"

"Maybe this is it," whispered Cy, excitedly rubbing at a spot with the sleeve of his shirt. "Here, give me your knife! It tooks like a cross chiseled in the surface of the stone!"

Delevan instantly produced a clasp knife and opened the blade.

Will dropped the almost raised bucket with a splash and they all crowded around to watch as Cy scraped away an accumulation of dust and dirt that had clogged the small x that was cut in the stone by some unknown surveyor.

A sigh of contentment left Delevan as he gazed at the mark. "By heaven, there she is! There's the mark, Cy! What do you say about Will Seven now?"

"He's a ringer!" ejaculated Cy, forgetting for the moment his animosity.

"Where's my compass?" asked Delevan as he searched through his pockets. "Ah, here it is, boys, let me put it down here on the mark. Now, let's see; we swing the compass around so the needle is over the North mark.

Now, fifteen degrees – no, thirty is what we want! Just sight along here and we get her in the sights, boys. Six hundred in the sights! Think of that!" He squinted across the face of the compass in the starlight and stood back gasping.

"What's the matter?" asked Storker, his thin face twisted with concern. "Hunh? What's the matter, Del?"

"It points right at the corner of our store," choked Delevan.

Will stared into the face of the bank robber, wondering what that could mean. He asked: "You mean the other well is under our store?"

"This ain't the mark," declared Cy, "and the only good thing about that is that I'm in $5,000 on the bet instead of out $100! Damn the luck! I was hopin' I lost!"

"No, by thunder – I see it now, Cy!" exclaimed the fat man, grabbing each of the others by the arm. "This is the right mark; it just means that the other well is closer to the wall of the bank than we thought. By golly, we're not far from the vault with the digging right now. You see, if you sight along the compass at thirty degrees east of north, the line intersects the corner of the store but continues on into the bank building, of course. And 115 feet must place it just about next to the building line! Get over there,

Cy, and make a mark on the wall where I tell you."

Storker ambled across the street and lounged next to the bank wall. He took out the makings and casually rolled a cigarette. Delevan gesticulated several times until Storker had rested his hand on the desired spot by pretending to lean on the wall with one hand as he lounged there. Delevan picked up his compass and walked slowly toward Storker, pretending, as he went, to engage Will in conversation, though in reality he was carefully pacing off the distance to the bank wall.

"Ninety-five feet," he murmured to them, after making a mental calculation to convert his paces into measurement. "Twenty feet from here, boys, is over half a million – waiting for us."

They laughed and went inside the store, closing the door and locking it securely. Delevan lowered the shades just as Cy brought the room awake with the glow of a lantern. The fat man smiled serenely at a passer-by as he lowered the last shade.

23.
In the Maze

Joyfully humming a little tune, Storker led the way down the ladder and into the cellar. More lanterns were lighted. With the help of Delevan they quickly established the new direction for the tunnel. Cy started to drill the holes from the existing tunnel, angling toward the bank vault.

They were so excited that they all took a turn at the drilling, and the work was done in a short time. Storker did the preliminary work with the blasting powder and fuses. More they could not do without firing the cannon.

They sat down and talked for some time before going to bed. Delevan pointed out that they were much closer to the vault than they had dared hope for; in fact they were lucky that their blasting had not been noticed more by the people in the bank. Cy estimated five blasts would bring them to the money. The last shot they decided upon firing when the cannon went off on the following Sunday at noon.

At last they extinguished the lanterns and climbed the ladder to go to bed. Will's mind was racing wildly as he tried unsuccessfully to fall asleep. There was, of course, the thought of the fortune waiting in the vault – his share being almost $200,000! There was also the thought of Dan Elgin and his smug countenance. There was the pretty face of Mary Elgin smiling at him and kissing him. As he slept at last, and dreamed, there was the demoniacal face of Lee Costain floating around him – bodiless, it seemed; there was, too, the angry vision of Fred Strate with his bandaged nose. He did not sleep well.

Dan Elgin was an early riser. In fact it was this habit to which he gave most of the credit for his personal success. He had found that the early bird got more than the worm. On the day following Will's visit to the ranch, he was at the bank even earlier than was his usual practice. He had checked his rig and team at the livery stable and was making his daily walk from that establishment to the bank building when he found his path crossing that of Will Seven. Evidently Seven was coming from the restaurant in the hotel across the street.

The meeting pleased Elgin for several reasons. First of all, he was impressed that

Seven also appeared to be an early riser. Second, he was most eager to talk to Will regarding the $20,000 reward money that was in the bank in Gaffert. Elgin envisioned investments for Will that could be profitable for both of them. Third, he regarded the former bum as an excellent suitor for the hand of his daughter. Beaus with a cash reserve of $20,000 were not common in or about Three Wells. Fourth, he regarded Seven as being sharp enough to guard the fortune that Dan was amassing and that would someday become the property of his only child and kin – Mary.

While all these things had entered his mind, it was the $20,000 that occupied the primary position. He fully believed that the way to bring the money to Three Wells was by befriending the boy.

As for the episode of the day before on the porch, he clung to the idea that he had not been outdrunk by the other but rather that something else he had partaken of had not agreed with him. Because he did not relish the idea that the drinking power of Seven was that much greater than his own, he dismissed the idea. Nor did he expect trickery, for he was sure that in that department, at least, he was more than the master of a youth such as Seven.

Elgin was not blind, however, to the fact

that his daughter was a more than normally passionate girl. After all, she was of his blood, and he could remember his own youth clearly enough. This was all the more reason why he feared for the loss of his wealth should the girl fall into the hands of some romantic fortune hunter. Seven, he admitted to himself, was the type of fellow who could hold the girl in check.

As they came close, with Will crossing the street toward the gunshop, Elgin smiled and hailed him.

"Oh, Will. Will Seven, good morning, lad – up early, I see."

Will stopped short, stepped up on the board sidewalk, and leaned against a wall of the bank. He answered: "Good morning, sir." Politeness was desirable.

"Now, now, Seven. None of that 'sir' business with me! You know my name – use it, boy. We're friends, aren't we? You might say drinking friends, eh?" He winked at Will and slapped him on the shoulder.

"Well – of course, Mr. Elgin if you –"

"No, no, no! Not Mr. Elgin, not to you, Will. Just call me Dan." Elgin smiled.

"Well, it seems funny," began Will, "a poor fellow like me calling you, the president of the bank, by his first name."

"Tut, tut, lad, come into the bank; I want

181

to have a few words with you." He took a small gold-colored key from his vest pocket and opened the door.

Will hesitated.

"Come on, Will, come right in," invited Elgin, holding the door for him.

Will entered the room and Elgin swung the door closed. It was very cool inside, for the heat of the morning had not yet penetrated the walls. Several of the shades on the side of the building were drawn, shutting out the morning sunshine. The front blinds were not drawn, however, and a light still burned near the door at the rear of the room that led to Dan Elgin's famous underground vault.

"Nice, isn't it?" purred Elgin, looking proudly about him.

"What?" asked Will, absentmindedly.

"I say, the bank is nice, isn't it?" Elgin frowned.

"Why, it don't look like a bank at all," said Will, looking about the room. "Where's the guard platform? Where's the vault? Where do you keep the money? In your desk?"

Elgin smiled. "You mean, you never heard about my vault? Why, my vault is known up and down this range as the safest place in the world for money!"

"Nope. I'm sorry Mr. Elg – er, Dan. I'm sorry, but I never heard anything about your vault. What's so special about it? Is it invisible? I don't seem to see it here," said Will, enjoying the fun of feigning ignorance of the famous vault.

"Listen, Seven," said Elgin, his voice showing just the slightest trace of irritation, although it was obvious that his pride was fiercely stung, "listen – you mean to stand there and tell me that you never heard about my well-vault and maze? Why, son you're joking! This bank of mine is known for a thousand miles around here."

"What maze?" asked Will with a blank expression.

"By thunder, you haven't heard," murmured Elgin.

"Your vault is hidden in a maze, eh? Damnedest thing I ever heard of. How do you find it?" asked Will. "Funny thing: back in New York they put the vault right out where you can see it. It's a darned hard thing to get any money out of one of them, though – maze or no maze!"

"By thunder, sometimes you say the simplest things –" began Elgin; then, checking himself: "How'd you like a job guarding this bank? You're the type I could trust. You could have your money sent down here and then you could keep an eye on it as well!"

"I think I could keep an eye on it better if it was in Gaffert," answered Will.

"How in the hell –" began Elgin, staring at Will.

"I mean that this maze of yours – money could disappear through a thing like that."

"It never has yet," boasted Elgin.

"Well, there's a first time for everything!"

"Not in this bank, Will. Listen, this bank is breakproof. This is the safest bank in the United States. Every cent that's locked in this bank is set in solid rock – surrounded on every side by rock, mind you! The lid on my vault has one of the best combinations ever devised. Besides, bank robbers hit and run. Look at any of the successful jobs that have been pulled. Just fit one of the accounts you read of into my maze down cellar, and see how impossible it would be for anybody to break this bank! Listen, Will" – he lowered his voice to a whisper – "the thing about this bank that makes it such a tough nut is this: not one soul in this world knows exactly where the vault of mine is – in the building, I mean: Come on, I'll show you why."

Elgin led the way to the rear door.

Will followed the banker, saying: "If this vault is so safe, what's the idea behind this maze of yours?"

"Just a little idea of mine, is all," said

Elgin, smiling over his shoulder. "I built this all by myself. I bring people down here once in a while and lead them around and then take them right up to the vault. I love to watch the expressions on their faces when they start to get turned around and lose their bearings."

"It seems like a lot of work," said Will, looking at the walls of the corridor they were in now.

Elgin turned right at the bottom of the stairs and led Will through a door, unlocking as he went. They reversed direction then, heading back in the direction opposite to the stairway. They proceeded some twenty feet, and turned to the left through another door that was adjacent to two others exactly like it in every detail. Elgin unlocked it with the same key. He replied, "Look, Will, the vault is in solid rock – right?"

"So you've said."

"Well, that seems safe enough in itself. Still, rock isn't steel, is it?"

"No."

"Well, then the rock could be broken into, couldn't it? I mean, supposing – just supposing, because this is just a fantastic notion of mine – suppose somebody tunneled right up to my vault underground."

"That's impossible!" exclaimed Will.

"Of course, but did you ever hear of a

185

prisoner tunnelling out of prison, through solid rock?"

"Why, yes, now that you mention it, I've heard of a couple of cases like that –"

"Sure," interrupted Elgin. "There was that case during the war, for one."

"I remember hearing about that," said Will.

"Well, Will, believe it or not, that's been my one fear for this vault. It's one in a million that anyone would ever attempt a thing like that. Still, this will show you what a careful man I am: I've taken care of that million-to-one shot with this maze of corridors and doors."

"I hardly think anyone –" began Will.

"You're right. You're absolutely right, Will. Nobody would try it because I'm always on guard. I'm always watching what's going on around here. Of course, nobody can figure this thing out – I get lost myself down here sometimes. I'll have you mixed up in a minute. You see, this way I can bring anybody down here and they still can't get any idea of where the damn vault is. Of course, by the time bank robbers found their way through here the town would be swarming around their ears!"

They passed down the corridor and came to one door at the end and one to the left and one to the right. They passed through the end door and came to an identical set of doors ahead of them within fifteen feet. This time Elgin unlocked the door on the left. They entered a new corridor, and Elgin paused to turn up a lamp.

This new hall had only one door leaving it, and that was on their right. As they entered this door, Elgin turned up another light and struck a match to the wick. This room was as small as a closet and, like so many of the others, had three doors. They went through the one on their right, finding themselves turning a corner and going through another door that brought them into a long narrow corridor with three doors at each end. This set of doors, like all the others, was at right angles.

Will laughed.

"Pretty good, eh?" giggled Elgin.

"I'm lost," confessed Will, though in reality he thought he still knew in which direction the back of the bank was and his approximate location. He fought to keep the twists and turns clear in his mind. He hated the thought of another turn, for he feared that then he would really be mixed up.

"You haven't started to get lost yet," predicted Elgin, and he led the way to the set of doors on their left. They went straight

187

through the door at the end. Once through the door they turned left again, and Elgin paused to take a lantern from a peg.

A single door awaited them at the end of that corridor, but they passed through it to a room with three doors that was so small there was scarcely room for the doors to open. Elgin opened a door and led the way with his lantern; the door swung closed behind them; they turned left and then right, and Will found himself staring at the big black shiny cover of the vault. The combination dial stared at him like an eye in the half-light of the lantern.

Will whistled.

"What's the matter?" asked Elgin, holding up the lantern to see his face better.

"I'm not only lost – I'm sick trying to figure out how to get out of here." Seven grinned.

"It affects some people that way," chuckled Elgin. "I almost went crazy down here every Sunday building this thing."

"I don't know how you did it," commented Will.

"Want to see the money?" asked the banker, his eyes glowing in the lantern light.

"Sure."

Elgin set the lantern down and spun the dial. He crouched over it to shut out the vision of the other. He paused for a second,

188

then, hearing a rewarding click, raised the cleverly counterweighted cover.

They gazed down at the drawers and stacks of money all neatly piled there. There were a number of individually locked boxes that evidently were Elgin's version of safe-deposit boxes.

"It's all mine. It's all mine," Elgin chuckled. "Well, most of it, anyway. Someday I'll get it all if they just give me time," he confided. "Would you like to get right down there, Will?"

"Some other time maybe. Let's get out of here," answered Seven, glancing back at the door.

24.
An Element of Doubt

As Will racked his brain for the next two days, trying to discover the secret of Elgin's passages, Delevan and Storker fired two more cannon shots and came still closer to the vault.

Elgin was more insistent than ever in his quest to get Will to take a job guarding the bank, especially when he found that the duties of Seven in the gunshop were little more than watching the store while Delevan and Storker were gone.

Storker worked like a fiend in the tunnel, taking all his meals in the cellar and never coming out. His absence was explained as a buying trip upstate to purchase a new brand of repeating rifle.

As regards his one trip through the maze, Will was completely stumped, and unable to solve the riddle of the doors and passages. Whenever they had a moment together, they would always find Seven asking about their trip through the maze. They had been equally perplexed, and the more so because the maze was a surprise they had not expected. There was only one clue as far as Will was concerned – only the last door had closed by itself. All the others Elgin had either pushed or pulled closed behind them, a fact that Delevan and Storker did not even recall from their visit.

On Thursday Will took the job as bank guard, the secret of the passages still haunting him. Elgin was overjoyed at the prospects of getting Will away from Delevan, but he didn't offer to take the youth through the passages again, preferring to have him just lounge about the lobby of the bank and talk to the customers. Elgin tried to explain certain facets of the business to Will.

On Thursday night they had supper at the Elgin Ranch, and Will found himself embarrassed as he confronted Mary. He drank enough of Elgin's whisky to find himself promising to wire Joe Becker to send his money down from the bank in Gaffert. He was trapped in the parlor this time, and had nowhere to dump the whisky. Elgin got the promise from the youth before succumbing to the effects of the liquor himself.

After dinner he found himself walking with Mary, and fighting off the lightning advances of the girl, who was as determined in her wants, it seemed, as was her father in his. They differed only in the ultimate object in their dogged insistence. Because Mary, of course, was beautiful and desirable, it was not surprising that they should find themselves sitting in the grass beneath one of the shade trees.

"Stop it."

"Stop what, Honey? Stop what, Will?"

"Stop kissing me like that."

"Why?"

"You don't know me well enough – that's why!"

"I know you all it takes."

"Whatta you mean?"

"I love you – I want to marry you, silly," she purred.

"Don't say that. I can't ever get married – not yet."

"Why?"

"I don't know, I just can't, Mary. Take your hand out of my hair; your mussin' it all up."

"I like it."

"Listen, you don't know me. You just think you know me; I'm a drifter; you're a million miles above me. You can have any guy on the range. What do you want with a bum like me?"

"You've got gray eyes," she reasoned.

"Lotsa guys have gray eyes!"

"Not like yours," she said, snuggling close.

"Whatta you mean?"

"Yours say things."

"What kind of things?"

"Like love."

Will choked. "Listen, Mary, I'm practically a crook; that's what I am. You don't know what a rat I am. I'm not the marrying kind."

"I don't care; I'll take you anyway."

"Don't say that."

"I mean it . . . kiss me a little. . . . Let's run away tonight. Let's get a couple of horses and run away, Will."

"Oh, Gawd, Mary, you don't know what you're saying. You'd be going with a bum, a crook – why, I'm the kind of a guy that could

192

rob your father's bank – think of that."

"I'm the kind of girl that could help you. Do you have a plan?" She stared up at him, her eyes earnest.

"You mean it, eh?"

"From the bottom of my heart," she declared.

"I can't figure it out," groaned Seven, drawing her close.

"I love you, Will. I love you. I love you, and that's it. If you're a crook, I'll be one, too. We'll have a whole family of crooks if you want."

"Stop it!" he cried, jumping up. "Don't talk like that, Mary!"

"I mean it," she said, standing with him. She looked up into his face.

"Mary, you're crazy!"

"In love," she admitted, wrapping her arms around him.

"You'd even help me be a crook, eh?"

"I'd wear a gun," she declared.

"You're not like any girl I ever knew," he said.

"Good."

There was a long silence as they held each other; presently she spoke:

"You're not like anybody I ever knew," she said.

"Why not?"

"You're a big nerve, Will Seven. A regular quivering muscle I can feel when I touch you. You're different, somehow – like a wild animal. You don't look wild, but I can feel it when I touch you. Oh, you're wild all right – or evil – or good – or something; but whatever this thing is that you are, I want to be made part of it. I want to be part of you, Will. I want to be controlled by you. Are you a crook, honey? God, I'll love you all the more, I think. Are you a crook?"

"I don't know, Mary," he groaned. "Damn it, I don't know!"

25.
Joe Becker

Delevan wandered up and down before the counter of the gunshop. He kept going to the window and staring out. He turned frowning toward Will, who lounged in one of the chairs. It was early morning.

Delevan said: "I don't know what the hell he's doing here. He's here, is all, and asking around about you. Says he's got a draft on the bank in Gaffert for $20,000 to give you!"

194

"That's all right, I suppose," murmured Will. "Still, how'd he know I was here? I just telegraphed him – unless – no, I don't think Elgin was sure enough of himself to do it yesterday. You're sure it's Joe Becker, hunh?"

"I know Joe Becker," nodded Delevan. "I've seen him twice before, but he don't know me, as far as I know. By God, Seven, this has a bad light to it! What the hell do you suppose he came 'way down here for?"

"How'd he come?"

"By train, brought his horse, too; left the train at Three Mile Creek water stop."

"That figures," said Will.

"Why?"

"It's the shortest way. Joe Becker's smart."

"There he is. You better get out there and talk to him; he's coming out of the telegraph office now. Go out the back way."

Will looked out the window first, and hurried out the back door. As he hurried along, his mind was spinning, for it was indeed Joe Becker in the street.

Joe Becker was a famous man. His diet was crooks, and he could smell one miles away. A person didn't have to be long in that part of the range to start hearing of the exploits of Joe Becker and his brothers.

Will had learned enough from listening to

195

the idlers and loafers in Delevan's gunshop virtually to write a biography on the lawman. Perhaps this was because the people of Three Wells knew that Will had been a prime mover, together with the big lawman, in the catching of Lee Costain. Therefore it seemed that on every occasion, whether he was at the gunshop or at his new duties in the bank, people would just naturally wander up to him and start talking about Joe Becker.

Joe was a giant not only in reputation but in actual physical size as well. He had two brothers that he employed as deputies, but they never attained his great stature or his reputation, though perhaps in many communities they would have been feared men.

Becker was sheriff not only of the county in which Gaffert and Cleary were located but of the county to the south as well. This second county included Three Wells. There were two reasons why Becker held both jobs. First, it was double pay; second, one county couldn't provide enough work for him. So he roamed up and down that part of the range, smashing in heads and shooting crooks as required. He was fast on the draw, and people said that his move for a gun could be timed to represent a quarter of a heartbeat. Generally it was the last heartbeat for those he drew against.

News of a new crook or an unsolved crime would send him hunting for that local at his first convenience, which was generally fifteen minutes after he heard the news. His office was in his saddlebags, for he ranged too far and wide ever to put his feet up on a desk. He generally brought his prisoners to the nearest jail, if he took them at all. He preferred for the most part to shoot them dead on sight, thus saving the county countless thousands of dollars in expensive trials.

Joe was well liked by the politicians, for his prudent habit gave them the opportunity to squander money that would ordinarily go for prison tenure. Joe's methods were so universally known to the outlaws in that area that they just naturally drew when in his presence, for it was kill or be killed. And Joe had never lost a draw.

People loved to tell about the time he had shot and killed the president of the Cleary Bank and the mayor of the same town. It was retold that Joe killed the banker with one shot in the heart and split the eyes of the mayor so quickly that the booming of his big Colt in the streets of Cleary was reported as one long explosion. Needless to say, this killing caused a good deal of consternation until Becker showed those present that the banker had a small derringer tucked in his palm.

At twenty yards Becker had seen it, and had done his shooting on one of his famous hunches that were never wrong – or so it was said. The town of Cleary was up in arms over the double killing until Becker quickly proved beyond all reasonable doubt that the two were planning to abscond with the bank's funds. It seemed that the assets of the bank were small in comparison with the deposits of the townspeople. Because of the exposure of the dead men and the crime they had planned, no word or action of Joe Becker was ever again questioned in Cleary. When he met someone and started shooting, that other person was immediately condemned in the eyes of the town. The dead bodies were buried unceremoniously in boot hill. Everyone loved Joe.

As Will came around the corner he was instantly spotted by Becker. The lawman changed his direction in midstride and immediately started toward Will.

"Howdy, Seven. Here's something for you." He handed Will a slip of paper.

" 'Lo Becker. What's this?"

"That's a draft on the bank in Gaffert for your reward money," declared Becker, stopping and standing with his arms folded.

"This piece of paper is my $20,000, eh," said Will dubiously.

198

"It's *good*, Seven."

"You didn't have to ride all the way down here to give me this, Joe," said Will, smiling.

"I didn't, but I was coming and I heard you were here so I brought it along."

"How come you're down here?"

"Business."

"Oh."

Becker eyed Will keenly.

"Whatta you wanta know for, Seven?"

"Why, nothing Joe; just askin', is all."

"Whatta you doin' here, Seven?"

"Mindin' my own business," said Will.

"Yeah, and what business is that?"

"I work at the bank."

"That so? That's a funny place for a high-flyer like you to spend time."

"I'm the guard," declared Will.

"Whatta you know about this new store over here?" Becker pointed to Delevan's.

"Oh, that's Delevan's gunshop."

"I can read. Who is this Delevan, anyway?"

"I haven't known him long," said Will.

"Long enough to just live there, eh?"

"What's wrong with that?" asked Will defensively.

"Is this Delevan a big fat slob?"

"He's pretty heavy," admitted the other. "Why?"

"Just wondered."

199

"You stayin' with us long, Joe?"

"Long as it takes, Seven, long as it takes."

"I see. Well, maybe you'll get to meet Delevan, then."

"What's his first name?" asked Becker.

"Why, Joe, now that you ask, I don't ever recall anyone callin' him by a name other than Delevan. Just plain Delevan is what he goes by."

"I hear he has a partner, a thin guy – a sort of weasel-face."

"That sounds like Storker to me." Will laughed.

"Storker, hunh? Storker, hm-mm. That name is familiar, but damned if I can recall where or what I heard about it. Think I'll just amble over and have a talk with this guy Storker."

"Can't do that."

"Why not?"

"He's upstate buying guns."

"Whereabouts upstate? What town?"

"Why – er, I don't know exactly where," stammered Will.

"You live with them but you don't know where, eh?"

"They said something about it but I didn't pay any attention. Just north of here, is all I know."

"You work at the bank, eh?"

200

"That's right, Joe."

"Well, Seven, being as it's Saturday, and being as you work at the bank, it would be a good idea to deposit that draft, don't you think?"

"That's just what I was gonna do."

"You were, eh? You got a lotta faith in that bank, don't you, Seven? You kinda like banks, don'tcha? You know, Seven, you're the first guy I ever knew to pass up steppin' up and collectin' twenty grand at the pay-off window. That sticks in my mind against you, Seven. 'Why,' I keep saying to myself, 'why does a gent walk past twenty grand?' That sure has caused me to lose a lot of sleep lately."

"I told you to put it in the bank," reminded Will.

"That's right, and that much is in your favor, kid – but, frankly, you smell like a crook to me. You saved my life, Seven, but that doesn't mean a damn thing to Joe Becker."

"That's good, Joe," said Will, rocking back and forth on his feet. "That's good because all of a sudden you don't smell so good to me – in fact, you stink!"

Becker drew back his head, and smiled. It was clear that he hadn't expected the retort. "Funny," he murmured, almost to himself,

"I never expected you to open up like that."

"You don't scare me, Becker – I pulled Costain off your neck, and I remember the look in your eyes!"

"Scared?"

"Yeah, scared."

"I suppose you been shootin' your mouth off like that all over town, hunh?"

"Not a word."

"Yeah, well that's good, Seven, because Costain is headed this way. He busted out over a week ago!"

Will staggered back as though struck.

"Costain got away? But that's impossible – we would have heard!"

26.
Change in Strategy

"I wouldn't let the word out. Nobody escapes from Joe Becker, Seven. I'll get him and drag him back to Gaffert on a rope! Costain is headed this way – that much I know. I took the train and beat him. When I heard he was comin' this way I got to thinkin' about you ag'in, Seven. You fit in this somewhere.

I'll shoot your heart out if I get the chance, you crook!"

"You're crazy, Becker!" exclaimed Will. "You're a lunatic!"

"You think you made a fool of me, Seven," snarled Becker, his face growing red. "You didn't, though. You trapped yourself! I turned Costain loose deliberately – though the fool thinks he escaped. I sent him down here to kill you – and he'll do it too; and then I'll shoot his ugly heart out."

He stepped back from Will and, turning abruptly, walked off up the street. Will stood staring at his broad back; the last words of the sheriff had taken him aback. He was sure Becker had detected the look of fear that mention of Costain coming to Three Wells had given him.

Will walked to the gunshop and, disdaining the rear entrance, headed toward the front door. He could see the head of Delevan anxiously bobbing in the window. He waved at the crook and turned, going instead to the bank, which had just opened. He could see that his change in direction upset the fat man, but he kept going.

Elgin's smiling face greeted him as he entered the bank.

"Good morning, Will. Joe Becker is in town with a draft for you, I hear."

"That sure is funny," said Will. "I just wired him yesterday; apparently he never got the wire, but was headed here with it, anyway. Er – did you get any other news from Becker?"

"Not to speak of," said Elgin. "Let's see the draft."

"Here it is. Cash it for me, will you?"

Elgin glanced at him. "You want to see it in the form of cash, eh?"

"Yeah."

"Very well, my boy; it won't take but a minute. Just a moment now." Elgin began counting out large bills onto the counter. The counting took some time. Presently he looked up and smiled at the two stacks before him, each containing $10,000. "There you are, son. Makes some sight, doesn't it?"

Will reached for the piles, but Elgin put out a restraining hand. "Just a minute, Will. You can't just take $20,000 and stuff it in your shirt and go walking around, you know."

"I can't? Why not?"

"Because somebody might knock you on the head and steal it. Besides, it'll be perfectly safe here in the bank. After all, you're the guard. I'll just give you a receipt for it!"

He whisked the piles out of sight, wrote out a receipt, and handed the paper to Will with a smile.

204

Will looked at it and said, "Another piece of paper!"

"It's as good as gold!" Elgin smiled.

"It's still just a piece of paper," said Will disappointedly, looking at it.

"Listen, Will, we'll take that money of yours and make it grow. Did you ever see money grow?"

"I was never close to it long enough," said Will, stuffing the paper into his pocket.

"We'll take $10,000 of your money and put it in a little deal I know of," said Elgin. "There's virtually no risk involved – I wouldn't steer you wrong. We'll double that ten, and then we'll take twenty of the thirty you'll have – where you going, Will?"

"I'll be back," said Will. "I don't feel too good."

Will left the bank and headed once more for the gunshop. As he stepped through the door, he was greeted by a perspiring Delevan.

The fat man wiped the sweat from his brow and said: "Why didn't you come back here? What the hell is Becker doin'? But never mind that; we've got trouble – real trouble. Cy has run into a granite boulder!"

"Is that all?" asked Will, looking blankly out the window.

"Don't be funny, Seven. There's a time for jokes."

"Lee Costain is comin' down too," said Will, his voice calm.

"So what? – *What* did you say?"

"I said Lee Costain is on his way here. Becker says he let him out deliberately; Becker is wise to something."

"God, we've got to get moving!" groaned Delevan, wiping his brow again. "Let's go down in the cellar and talk to Cy. Hang the closed sign on the door and lock it."

Delevan hurried to the back room. Will followed him, first closing the shop.

They went down the ladder. Will saw that the cellar was now heaped so high with rock that very little space was left. A light shone from the tunnel. As they approached, the gaunt face of Storker poked through the opening. He was covered with fine dust.

"It's bad, boys, real bad. We're right up there except for this damn boulder. Imagine running smack into a piece of granite in limestone. It's a freak of nature. I never seen anything like it yet."

"What'll we do?" asked Delevan, wiping his brow with his big red handkerchief.

"We'll need about three more days," declared Cy.

"That's out," murmured Will.

"Why? Why is it out? Are you givin' the orders now?" asked Cy.

"Because Lee Costain and Strate and some of their gang are heading for us, Cy," explained Delevan.

Cy sat on the stone rubble with a loud groan and stared at them unbelievingly. "That's murder!" he exclaimed.

"It's apt to be," commented Delevan. "Well, at least we have a warning. I wonder how long we have? Do you suppose he'll get here before tomorrow night?"

"If he does we're sunk," said Will.

"Then there's Joe Becker to think of," murmured Delevan.

"Joe Becker? My Gawd, did you say Joe Becker?" asked Cy, gulping visibly, his large Adam's apple bobbing.

"He's already here," said Will.

"He is?" asked Storker, turning to Delevan for confirmation.

Delevan nodded.

"Oh, brother, I knew things were going too good. Well, there's only one thing to do: dynamite the hell out of that rock tomorrow and hope it drops clear. If it don't, if it just comes back a foot or so, Dan Elgin will sure as hell spot it Monday morning, and the jig is up."

"Maybe we'll have to take a crack at things from the other side, Cy," said Delevan. "Maybe we better plan on just bustin' in and trying to blow the lid off the vault."

"We could do it, too," commented Cy. "Will here has a key to the bank. We could go downstairs and open doors until we found the way into that vault. By Gawd, I'll spend the rest of the day making soup out of this dynamite we have left!"

"Cy is right, of course; it would be well to be ready for anything in case something goes wrong in the tunnel," said Del. "Maybe we oughta blow the rock out tonight."

"With Becker in town?" asked Will. "Why, he'd be here in a minute. No, it'd be better to wait for the cannon shot; that'll cover the noise of the blast. Besides, Sunday is a better day to do it. That new widow over in Rebel Hill is still drawin' everybody over to the church – I hope." There was silence following this remark until Will added: "Or maybe we oughta pull out and forget the whole thing. We'd at least get off with our necks. Costain ain't gonna be nice when he sees me."

"Don't think he loves us," declared Storker glumly. "But it's Becker that worries me – he's got more lives than a cat."

"I don't feel like giving up now," said Delevan. "Six hundred thousand steels up my nerve some. Facing Costain won't be easy, but I ain't afraid of Lee, and he knows it. Becker is the turn I can't take. How about you, Will?"

"I'm not afraid of him. He's real fast like they say, eh?"

"Like streak lightning," said Storker, hugging his knees up to his chest as he stared at Seven.

"Say, Del," began Will, "you ain't gonna take the money that's in those private boxes, are you?" Will stared at the outlaw.

"Money is money, Will. I'll add anything to Elgin's hoard that we can carry out with us. The first thing we'll do when we get in that vault is scoop up all the loose stuff and throw it in the bag, see? Then if things are going good, we smash the locks on those boxes and toss in the private stuff. We always do it that way, don't we, Cy"

"That's right," Storker grinned. "Oh, there's some beautiful piles socked away in those boxes. Probably another $100,000 in a bank this size, eh, Del?"

"At least," confirmed the fat man with a nod.

"But a lot of that belongs to widows and old people and people who saved it up with hard work and sweat!" protested Will.

"No difference, Will. No difference at all. Elgin will get it all, with his damn interest and such, before he's done. We'll just speed up the process. Elgin is a businessman, see; that means he's out to do all these people in if he can. So really, when you think about it, we're just stealing from the banker. At least, that's how I always think of it when I'm spendin' the stuff."

"Why sure," said Cy; "actually, we're doing those people a favor. This way, they'll have time to start working and build up another nest egg before they die. Elgin would have it all by the time they got senile anyway. We're just doing Elgin out of some business, you might say."

"That's a hell of a hard way of looking at it, Cy," declared Will, staring hard.

"Listen to him!" howled Cy. "He's scared all of a sudden – scared of some old widow. What'll he do when he runs into Joe Becker's Colt spitting lead?"

"I'm not scared of that!" said Will hotly.

"You're scared and you're stupid, Seven!" ejaculated Cy. He added: "Gawd, you were sure behind the door when the guts was passed out!"

"By golly, that's it!" exclaimed Will, jumping up.

"That's what?" asked Delevan, turning.

"That's the reason I couldn't figure that damn maze out! Why, it's as simple as hell. That last door closed by itself."

"What the hell is he talking about? Is he daft?" asked Storker, looking at the fat man.

"Quiet, Cy. What *are* you talking about, Will?" asked Del.

"There were four doors at that last turn," said Will. "One of them swung out and covered the door to the vault. The door to the vault was behind one of the other doors when Elgin swung it open. That's how he fooled me and everybody else! I remember seeing him smirk at the time we passed through – the old fox. There's a spring on that door, and it closed after us. That's how he could step ahead and know I wouldn't spot it. He led us through that same spot twice. By golly, I could go right to that vault on one try, now."

"Why, I remember that turn too," said Delevan, suddenly brightening. "This makes it a little easier; if the stone don't move, we'll go in and blow the lid!"

Storker dashed into the cellar and danced about excitedly. "We'll do better than that, by Gawd! We'll set a charge in the lid and pop it off at the same time we fire the cannon. We'll fire all three charges at the same time and be inside that vault scooping up happiness just like we planned!" He continued: "Will, you'll have to get me down to that vault tonight, though!"

"I can't do that. I have to see Mary

211

tonight," said Will.

"To hell with Mary, kid – she'll wait. The money'll buy a thousand Marys."

Will rushed at Storker and grabbed him by the throat. "Take that back, you – you croaker," he blurted.

"He's chokin' me," gasped Storker. "Ugh – he's killin' me. Del, hold him back he's – ugh!"

"Stop it! Stop it!" shouted Delevan.

Will released his grip, for he had not heard Delevan speak in such a tone of authority before. He turned to Delevan. "All right, Del. I'll get you into the bank. Then I'm getting out of here. *I quit!* I'm going away with Mary – if she'll come. I don't want *any* of the money. To hell with it!"

"Suit yourself, Will," said Delevan, smiling. The increased split apparently was sufficient consolation to the fat man.

27.
Saturday Night

The rest of the day was a torment to Will. He returned to the bank and finished out his stint, but he spent all his time lost in thought. He wanted to write a note to Mary and send it along with Elgin to the ranch. However, because he feared that the banker would read the contents, he refrained from doing so.

He was supposed to go to the ranch with Elgin, but he made the same excuse that he had this morning, telling Elgin that he did not feel at all well and would be out the following day. He felt some strange loyalty to Delevan and Storker – but for what reason he did not know. Perhaps he thought that it was only through them that he had met Mary, whom he knew he loved. Had they not interfered that day of the fight with Elgin's crew, he would never have met her. He planned to leave Three Wells immediately after leading them through the maze. The success of the rest of the venture they would have to bear. He justified his act by telling himself that he would not actually be taking any of the money. All he had done was to get the paper from Costain and find the hidden bench mark. Was that a crime? What was wrong with taking a slip of paper from an outlaw – a known train robber, at that? And for that matter, the prying of the bench mark from Elgin was no crime. No matter how the two crooks broke into the vault, Elgin would probably never learn that the bearing

213

had been used, or the bench mark either, for that matter.

He planned to head immediately for the Elgin Ranch to try to talk Mary into coming away with him on the spur of the moment. He thought she would. But if she refused, he would just keep riding – he still had Black Boy, and could put a thousand miles between himself and Joe Becker, who seemed determined to hound him to the end of the range, if necessary.

The fact that Becker would shoot him on sight at any time after the robbery gave an urgency to the thought that he must flee. He must not remain in this part of the country, even if Delevan and Storker were caught or, for that matter, were successful and escaped.

Going to the window and looking out, late that afternoon, as Elgin was closing the bank, Will was startled to see Becker lounging in a chair on the veranda of the hotel and staring in the direction of the bank. Apparently the lawman was going to maintain his vigil until something happened. Will cursed, but at the same time he was thankful that the sheriff hadn't tried to talk to Elgin about his suspicions.

The scene was peaceful enough to look at, but to Will the whole town was charged with electricity, and teetering, it seemed, on the

214

verge of an explosion. He jumped when Elgin came up behind him and said, "Starting to liven up a bit, isn't it, Will?"

"What?" said Will. "What is?" His voice broke slightly.

"The town – the town, my boy. It's Saturday night. I suppose you want to stay in town tonight and sow a few wild oats, eh? There, there, that's all right; I understand. A man doesn't want to become hog-tied too soon. I approve, for that matter. You'll be out for dinner tomorrow, of course. Don't worry; I won't say anything to Mary. You know, Will, things will be popping around here in a little while, and I'm half tempted to stay and have some fun with you!"

"I'd feel better if you were with Mary tonight – inasmuch as I'm not coming out," said Will.

"Well, I'm tired, and it has been a hard day. You won't regret putting your money in the bank, Will. A man has to set something aside for his old age, you know."

"You have to live a long time to be able to do that," said Will, staring out at Becker.

They left the bank and locked the door. Will purposely did not make a show of using his key; instead he let Elgin lock the door. Dan headed for the livery stable and his rig, and Will walked across the street to the

215

restaurant. It wasn't that he was hungry for he was so tense that he could do no more than drink a glass of water when he got there. Somehow he didn't want to go directly into the gunshop under the stare of Becker. Will lounged around the restaurant until dark, passing the time looking at some battered, out-of-date magazines.

He was just preparing to leave when Joe Becker stepped through the door and brushed past him, sitting down at the counter without greeting Seven.

"It's a funny thing," said Becker to the man behind the counter. "There's not a cloud in the sky, but I could swear that lightning was about to strike around here. Does it feel like there's electricity in the air to you?"

"Real peaceful is the way it seems to me," said the counterman.

Will left the restaurant. As he headed across the street, he saw six large horses standing at the rack before the salon. It was the time of night when the slicked-up cowboys, weary from the monotony of life on the range, rode in to drink whisky and dance with the girls in the saloons before going back for another week of drudgery in the hot sun. However, there was something about the horses that caused him to look twice, for they were gigantic brutes, probably all thoroughbreds – not the small mustangs that were more common in that locale.

One of the horses was a huge gray, a full two hands higher than any other horse there, although all were uncommonly big. The horses were a pretty sight, for they were covered with the sweat of a hard ride and steam was rising from their bodies in the cool night air. Will thought that the cowboys that rode them into town must have been in a great hurry to sweat the animals like that.

He used his key to let himself into the rear of the gunshop. Delevan hustled by him, coming from the front of the store. Will was surprised to see him still sweating, even though the cool of the evening had arrived. The fat man was in his shirt sleeves and vest, his shoulder holster openly showing. But his armament now went beyond the usual, for he had also donned crossed gun belts at his hips, and the big butt of another pistol protruded from above the belt of his pants where he had still another weapon tucked in his waistband. The rounded tip of a derringer butt gleamed from his vest pocket and he carried a shotgun in his hand.

"Holy cow! You goin' to war?" gasped Will, looking at the armament.

"Do something!" exclaimed Delevan. "They're here!" The fat man hurried to

217

the ladder, and disappeared.

Will followed, and as he started down the ladder asked: "Who's here? You mean Lee's in town?"

"They rode up about fifteen minutes ago," said Delevan, his voice a hoarse whisper. "Long Lee, the thin rat, Fred Strate, and four others I don't know. They're probably finding out plenty in the saloon right now." He turned to Storker, who was coiling out some fuse on the floor. "All set?"

"Just about," mumbled Storker, his voice suddenly shaking. "Damn fuse is all tangled up. When do you want to shoot it?"

"You two get over next door and pack the soup around the lid. I'll put out the lights and keep watch from the window. Hurry up, because Becker just went in and started to eat dinner. Don't let that fool see you, though, because he's got eyes in the back of his head. Go right in; don't hesitate no matter who sees you. 'He who hesitates is lost!' I'll have a rifle with a telescopic sight trained right on Becker's backbone. I can line him up where he's sitting, from the window here. If he makes one move to get up before you get out, I'll cut him in two!"

Will gulped at the finality with which Delevan spoke. The plan, it seemed, was now to go immediately ahead with the blast in spite

218

of the fact that the cannon could not logically be fired at this time of night without arousing great suspicion. If Joe Becker obeyed some impulse that jogged his nerves, he was to be shot dead – in the back. Will felt sorry for the big lawman. He hoped that the electricity the sheriff had mentioned did not cause him to stir from the stool at the counter while he ate his supper.

Storker seemed to have the fuse in order, and they climbed the ladder for what Will hoped was the last time. Storker paused to lift a package gingerly that contained the boiled-down dynamite – nitroglycerine, enough to blow the lid off Elgin's vault.

They stepped through the back door, and the last sight that Will saw as they passed into the darkness was the face of Delevan as he blew out the lamp.

They crept cautiously around the corner of the gunshop and paused to look up and down the street. Across the way they could hear the racket coming from the saloon. The windows threw bands of light into the street, and a large shaft of light shone from above and below the batwing doors. Across the street in the restaurant they could see the broad back of Joe Becker hunched over his plate.

Four cowboys rode into town with a whoop, and dismounted before one of the saloons farther down the street. For a second the street was completely deserted. It seemed too good to be true, yet Will's impulse was to turn and run for his life, straight back down the alley and out of the town. He felt as if he could run straight across the range and somehow, if he kept running long enough, escape or wake up from the horrible nightmare he was suddenly living.

Storker tugged at his sleeve, and they went quickly toward the door of the bank. Will fumbled with the key, then dropped it. Storker cursed and looked around. Seven picked up the key and tried in vain to get it in the lock. Had the lock been changed? Maybe Elgin was in league with Becker, and the lock had been altered. Will cursed.

"What the hell are you doin', makin' a new lock?" groaned Storker, glancing toward the restaurant. "I think Becker is gonna get it – I see his back twitchin', like."

The key slipped into the lock and the door swung open with a loud squeak. Will knew that the door squeaked, but somehow it had never seemed so loud before. They stepped inside, closed the door, and hesitated a moment to see if there was an alarm. Apparently they had entered without anyone seeing them.

They started for the rear door at a run,

expecting at any moment to hear the shot ring out that would kill Becker and end his career. Will unlocked the door and they hurried down the stairs. They hurried through the first four doors, lighting the lamps as they came to them. They avoided the first detour by entering the right door, and came out at once to the small closet-like room that appeared to have three doors. They squeezed past the door by opening one of the others; then they stepped back and Will swung the door closed, triumphantly revealing the hidden door with its spring hinges.

They unlocked the door and, turning the corner, came to the vault. Storker went to work on the lid with a flurry of movement and in no time at all he had the crack around the circumference of the heavy steel cover packed with the deadly nitro.

He began unwinding the fuse, working backward slowly on his hands and knees as he played out the length of it. Will walked ahead of him, opening the doors and clearing the way. There was an anxious moment as the door with the spring hinges closed and kinked the fuse. Storker cursed and spent several precious moments kneading and working the fuse to make sure it was not damaged. Satisfied, he continued his work. At first his hands shook, but unkinking the fuse calmed

221

him, and he moved with smooth confidence through the rest of the job. The remaining doors they left open. The great length of fuse went twisting and turning through the corridors with them. At last it played out at the bottom of the stairs.

With a sigh Storker stood up and looked at Will. He felt his pockets

"Got a match?" he whispered.

Storker never seemed to have a match when he smoked, and Will found himself about to deny that he himself possessed one. Perhaps it was yet not too late. Perhaps this was how the adventure would end – the scheme foiled for lack of a match.

Storker stared at Will, but getting no ready answer he quickly stabbed his hand into Will's vest pocket and brought out several matches. Cy scratched one along his pants. As it flickered alive, he stooped and lighted the fuse. They stood watching it creep slowly away from them. Will was surprised at how slowly it burned.

28.
Things Start Popping

Storker led Will up the stairs, taking them two at a time and on the run. They dashed through the bank, eager to get to the front wall and the protection of the space below the windows, for they were clearly visible in the light of the burglar lamp that always glowed in the rear of the room.

They dropped down on the floor, then cautiously looked out the windows. Across the way, Joe Becker was still talking with the counterman. As the big lawman waved his hand this way and that, apparently spinning some exciting narrative, Will expected to hear the glass shatter at any minute as Delevan murdered the man in cold blood. Cy jumped up and ran out the door, leaving Will to follow. Will slammed the door with a crash and dived most of the fifteen feet to the covering shadow of the alleyway; he landed on all fours and scrambled into covert. He slipped back to the edge of the walk and glanced up and down the street. Apparently all was well, for he could now see Joe Becker being served a second cup of coffee.

As he started through the door, Delevan almost knocked him down again as he went bustling outside with all the equipment that was used for firing the cannon. Besides the great assortment of firearms that he was carrying, he now had under his arm a bag of powder, a large bundle of wadding, a big powder horn and, of course, the ramrod.

"Where are you goin'?" asked Will, for with the sudden appearance of Lee Costain it seemed that everything had been speeded up to the point where each was thinking for himself and carrying out a separate plan. This seemed to be all the more true because they didn't even speak to one another; Storker went through the room and down the ladder at a rapid rate.

Delevan walked straight past Will without any reply and closed the door after him. Will could see by the expression on his face that the fat man was concentrating every energy on the coming crisis and the various ways of meeting it.

Will, forgetting that he had done the part he promised and was supposed to be on his way to the Elgin Ranch for a last-minute talk with Mary and an attempt to persuade her to come away with him, walked to the ladder and climbed down to see what Storker was doing.

He was suddenly aware that a great calm had come over him. He was no longer the person who had fumbled the key to the bank. It was as if he had somehow become detached from the whole scene and was watching players on a stage. He suddenly found himself feeling that the arrival of Costain was his fault. Strangely, he wanted to see Costain again. He found himself checking his Colt.

Storker was setting out another length of fuse.

"How do you know when the blast will go off, Cy?" asked Will, regarding the top of Cy's head.

Storker looked up. "That's easy. There's a hundred feet of fuse down there in the cellar; it burns ten feet a minute. It'll go off in ten minutes! Less than that now! I just keep looking at my watch and cut this fuse shorter. I can make both go off pretty close. You'd better get upstairs and see if you can be helpful."

Will started up the ladder, climbing quickly, for suddenly he felt trapped and wanted the freedom of the open air. He ran out the back door, pausing to pick up a rifle that leaned by the door. Delevan was in the alley, ramming home the charge of powder in the cannon. The noise of Will's approach caused him to pause in his work

225

and free one hand long enough to point the muzzle of a big Colt straight at the heart of Seven. Will skidded to a stop, for the look in Delevan's eye was that of a man about to kill without question.

The fat man said, "Oh, Will – it's you!"

He dropped the gun back into the holster and returned to his work of ramming into the open barrel of the cannon a large swatch of wadding. He jammed the pick into the touch hole, puncturing the wool cartridge. He threw the pick away and began pouring priming powder from the powder horn into the touchhole of the cannon.

He was not at all careful, as on other occasions, not to spill any of the priming powder; when the hole was filled he merely tossed the powder horn on the ground, with the contents momentarily flying in every direction.

Del leaned his shotgun against the wall and, turning to Will, said: "Come on and help me get her out to the street – quick now!" He bent to the task of rolling the wheel near him. The cannon started to move, and Will remembered for an instant how strong Delevan was.

Will dropped his rifle against the building and strained at the other wheel. They rolled the cannon out of the alley and into the street. A group of cowboys coming into town rode slowly by, watching curiously. Delevan saluted them by briefly touching his brow, then instantly returned to the work of turning the wheel. Apparently the cowboys saw nothing amiss in all this, for Delevan's cannon was famous, and would a man up to anything stop and greet anyone as casually as he had – with a smile, even?

Delevan and Will got the gun into the middle of the street. But Del's next action surprised Will, for the fat man struck a match along the rough surface of the barrel, stuck the match into the limstock, and ignited the powder at the touchhole. There was a hissing sound as it burned through the priming powder, and then a tremendous roar as the cannon went off. They both stood with their hands over their ears. The roar was tremendous, and Will realized that Delevan had used more powder than ever before.

The effect of the blast was instantaneous. Doors flew open all along the street; windows squeaked up, and shutters fastened earlier against the ravages of a typical Saturday night in Three Wells swung outward.

With the first show of heads in the windows and the first outpouring onto the porches by the citizenry, Delevan exclaimed in a huge voice, "Whoopee! Yippee!"

Across the street, in the restaurant, Becker leaped erect as though he had been shot in the back, and Will wondered if his famous intuition was at work now. Down the street in the saloon where Costain and his band were gulping down whisky to quench their thirst after their long ride, a score of heads clustered in the doorway. Two giants towered above the crowd – Strate and Lee Costain standing side by side and staring their way.

While Will had suspected that the blast would bring an aroused citizenry about their ears with cries of "Bank robbers!" nothing like that happened at all. In fact, the townspeople passed it off as a joke. This was obvious from the good-natured laughing and comments.

Will heard one man in his shirt sleeves call to another, "What is it?"

"Delevan," laughed the second man.

"Had a few drinks, I suppose," rejoined the first.

People were laughing all along the street. Delevan waved to them all.

"Shoot it again!" someone hollered.

Delevan waved, and turned to Will. "Run and tell Cy to touch off the blast!"

Without hesitating, Will turned and ran back into the alley, noting that the people were already going back into their houses,

228

calm in their assumption that it was all just horseplay and probably thinking that he was going for more powder. He was fascinated with the progression of events and with the knowledge that only he, Delevan, and Storker knew all that was about to happen. He had completely forgotten Mary and the wrong he was committing. He threw open the door and shouted, "Shoot it off, Cy!"

There was a curse from down below. Thinking of all the time that had elapsed while they struggled to get the cannon out into the street and fired, he realized that Cy would have to use an extremely short fuse.

A second, tremendous boom filled the air. The town remained strangely quiet this time as Will raced into the street and glanced around. This time the blast might not have meant anything to the townspeople, but Joe Becker was running from the door of the restaurant, a big black Colt in each hand.

From the saloon came a howl of delight from the drunken patrons, but six forms broke from the door on a dead run, heading into the street – the remnant of the Costain gang, and in the fore were the famous train robber himself, and Fred Strate.

"Lee!" screamed a voice from up the street to their left.

Will recognized the voice as that of

Delevan, and wondered how the fat man could have covered so much ground in the short time he had been gone.

The outlaws wheeled as one and turned toward the shout. Will surmised that Delevan's end had come. There was a chorus of curses as the outlaws opened fire.

Twin booms from a shotgun sent the group groveling in the dirt of the street, howling with pain and rage. Delevan had knocked down the whole Costain gang with two well-placed loads of buckshot. Out of the twisted mass of bodies two forms rose to their knees, firing blindly.

Becker stopped in his charge toward the cannon, and Will Seven stared in disbelief at the firing up the street. Becker ran toward the sound of the fighting, for in his heart of hearts that was where he longed to be – better to die in the midst of a ferocious shoot-out between two groups of crooks, or survive to bask in the glory of such an encounter. Will Seven, standing alone in the street, could be dealt with later. Joe ran toward the greater glory.

Storker flew past Will on the run, a big sack over his arm. Will watched the thin, shadowy figure dart along the sidewalk and into the bank building.

The third explosion ripped the night air – now punctuated by screams and pistol shots.

This, by far the largest blast of all, was the charge that Cy had set to loosen the granite boulder near the vault in the tunnel.

The second blast halted Becker, who had already shot two of the outlaws who were limping toward their horses. This third blast, reverberating up through the ground, he didn't understand. The outlaws, it seemed, were up ahead, fighting among themselves; yet the blast had come from behind him. Were there more men – perhaps successfully robbing the bank at this minute?

The thought turned him cursing back toward Will, shooting as he came.

Will turned and dashed around the side of the gunshop, away from the bank. Will paused and fired from cover around the corner. He was surprised when his wildly flung shot knocked the hat from Becker's head, causing the lawman to break stride. But Becker bore on, willing to take a bullet if he could still get to the alley and kill Seven.

Will dashed around the corner and the rear of the bank, running with all his might. When he came to the street, having circumvented the building, he dashed along the sidewalk and into the only cover available – the bank itself! Behind him he could hear the crashing footfalls of the heavy Delevan going down the stairs rapidly. The fat man had made it to the bank.

Will ran through the bank, terrorized at the wild charge of Joe Becker, who was running along the sidewalk with a rifle, apparently the one that Will had dropped in the alley when moving the cannon, levering shots off as fast as he could work the action. Will heard the terrible screaming of rifle slugs all around him as the bullets smashed the glass and tore at the wood in the room. Ten straight shots flew at him, and he dived for the stairway, going down head over heels and somehow managing to hold onto his pistol. He lay stunned at the bottom for what seemed like minutes, urging his body to move but getting no response.

He heard Becker upstairs cursing and reloading his pistols. Will crawled into the corridor with great effort and, once moving, began to feel himself again. The first sound of Becker's cautious step on the stair sent the adrenalin surging into his blood, and he ran down the corridor, slamming every door behind him.

There was silence as Becker crept down the stairs; then he heard the lawman shoot off the first lock and enter the first corridor full of doors with a curse. The lamps were turned down low, and the trail left by the fuse, a dead giveaway, was hardly visible.

There were more sounds on the stairs now, and Will's heart leaped as he stood pressed against the wall and heard the sound of Lee Costain's angry voice booming in the underground corridor. Strate, too, had made it into the bank.

Will wondered if anything could kill those two. There was a frightful curse ahead of him as Strate and Costain apparently ran into Joe Becker. A fusillade of shots rang out, along with several cries, but apparently no one was hurt, for no sound of pain came to Will.

"It's Becker! It's Becker!" screamed Costain.

"I think I got him!" shouted Strate.

A blasting of well-placed shots showed the futility of his thinking.

An answering salvo came from the two outlaws. Then another shot, and the splintering of a lock told Will that Becker had taken refuge behind the second door.

Will slammed the doors behind him and raced to the vault. Before him he could see the image of Mary's face floating in the dim light. He would never see her again, for no matter what the outcome of the fight behind him he would be branded as a robber and probably a murderer before the night was over. There would be no witnesses as to who killed whom.

He came to the vault to find Delevan and

Storker scooping bills into the bag. Delevan held the sack by the top as Storker gleefully threw money into it with both hands. Will thought that, had he been Joe Becker, they both would have been dead, so entranced were they with the wealth around them.

The cover of the vault was twisted in a grotesque shape – evidence of the skill of Storker with explosives. As Will glanced into the old well, he found to his surprise that the boulder had been removed by the huge blast from below and that a gaping hole revealed the tunnel. The light from the cellar of the gunstore showed through it. An idea flashed into his mind.

He leveled the pistol and said, "All right, you two – drop the bag!"

They stared at him aghast – frozen.

"Will, don't be a fool! You can't get away with it! There's enough here for all of us," panted Delevan.

"I don't want any," said Will.

"He don't want any!" repeated Storker, perplexed but still drunk with the sight of the money around him.

"You don't get it either, Cy. Drop your guns or I'll kill the two of you and take credit for catchin' you."

"He means it," moaned Storker, dropping his gun into the money.

Delevan stubbornly stood watching Will, his small eyes looking for some chink in the other's armor.

29.
"Give It to Me in the Guts!"

Will scowled at Delevan, for he could see that the fat man was waiting for the chance to draw his gun.

"Okay, Del, if you won't listen, go for your gun. I'll just shoot you in the belly. Of course, you can still get out and have a small profit besides. Take the reward for Costain – that's $20,000. Take your own $25,000 out too. Elgin can get his $5,000 loan back by selling your guns. Take $45,000 and get through the tunnel to some horse in the street. If you double around in back you can make it to Costain's horse, Bayard, out there at the rack by the saloon. Storker, you can get to Strate's horse."

"Are they dead?" asked Delevan.

"They're in the maze, trying to get Becker. If you wait a half minute longer, the town will

235

have this place surrounded and you'll have to dodge shotguns!"

Delevan looked at Storker.

"Why don't you make a try for him? You're fast!" coaxed Cy.

"Why didn't you," demanded Delevan, "instead of dropping your gun down there in the money?"

Will cocked his gun.

Delevan glanced at his belly. He smiled up at Will, looking for all the world like a cherubic boy, and said to Cy: "Quick, count out $45,000 – that seems the safest way out of this to me." Storker counted like mad, stuffed the money into his shirt and, glaring at Will, dived into the tunnel. Delevan backed through the opening, smiling as he went, and waved goodbye.

Will heard them as they climbed out of the cellar in the gunshop, and then, moments later, he heard the door slam. He turned back toward the maze and Joe Becker as several shots rang out. He could hear Fred Strate moaning. Apparently he had fallen before Becker's guns.

Will hurried through the false part of the maze, using his key deftly, for he did not want to show his presence by shooting the locks off the doors as the others were doing. He could hear them blasting away, and the

236

doors swinging wildly as they dived about, searching for cover. The sounds of Strate's moaning seemed to be coming from the back of the building.

Will came to the door that he was sure led to the main corridor through which the fuse had been laid. He paused to replace the spent shell in his gun.

"You got Fred, Becker – I'll kill you now!" screamed Costain.

"I'll meet you head on, you crook," answered Becker. "What do you keep jumpin' behind something for?"

"You're the one that's yellow," shouted Costain, laughing hoarsely. "Come on out and finish what you started, you yellow skunk!"

"Where are you?" hollered Becker, stung by the insult.

"Right here in the long room with all the doors," declared Costain.

"Where the hell is that? I'm lost – keep talking so I can find you," shouted Becker.

"Over here! I'm not lost, but you are. Ha! that proves how stupid you are, Becker – yi-yi!"

A series of explosions shattered the room on the other side of the door from Will. Two screams came to him, then silence.

Will opened the door a crack.

Becker was down at the end of the room,

slumped on the floor and holding his shoulder. One gun was empty it seemed, for he disdained to draw it. The other lay a few feet away, where it had fallen when the force of the bullet he had taken in the shoulder had knocked it from his hand. He groped for it.

Costain was shot in the leg, and blood poured from the wound. He was also shot in the head, or grazed, it appeared. There were a dozen patches of blood about the rest of his body where the initial buckshot charge of Delevan had knocked him down in the street. Yet in spite of all this he was drawing himself to his feet. He had a Colt in each hand and he was cocking them as he stepped down the corridor, his ugly, bloody face twisted with the pleasure of finishing his long-time antagonist on the side of the law.

"How do you want it, Becker? How do you want your last bullet?"

Becker stopped trying to reach his gun. He was beaten. As he drew himself up to face death, he said:

"Anybody can take it in the head, I suppose, or just have their heart blotted out by a slug, eh, Lee? Well, I've never taken the easy path. Why should I now? You want me to say, 'Make it quick,' or somethin' like that, don't you? To hell with you, Lee! Give it to me in the guts!"

238

"That's the way you want to go, eh, Joe, a bullet in the stomach, hunh?"

"Shoot!" said Becker, straightening.

"Here she comes, you lousy rat," screamed Lee, raising his gun.

"Look out, Lee, I'm behind you!" called Will, able to bear no more. He stepped through the door.

"What the –" began Costain as he turned with both guns spitting orange flame in the dim light.

"I got you! I got you!" howled Costain as Will was slammed back by the force of his bullets.

Then he looked down at the two geysers of blood pumping from each side of his own chest. "Gawd – I'm dead," he choked, blood in his mouth.

Will looked at his own wounds, then closed his eyes, and died.

He awoke in what was apparently the next world, for great cartwheels of fire were exploding and rolling about before his eyes. This new world was cooler, and he heard people talking all around him. He heard Becker's voice calling for a doctor. He lay for a long time like that, before he heard Mary sobbing at his side.

Everything was over for him. If he lived he

would go to jail, and that would be worse than dying. Perhaps he was a murderer, though he had killed no one except Costain.

He could hear Strate mumbling nearby, and then he heard Becker say:

"Well, I brought Seven out, but the fat guy and the other one got away on Costain's horses. They didn't get much, though. Most of the money's down there yet. At first I figured this kid was in on the deal – I even pegged a dozen shots at him – but he ran in the bank and scared off the other two. He had to, you see, because with me pinned down they had plenty of time to clean the place out. It woulda been the biggest robbery in the West! Then the kid come back and saved me, just as Costain was gonna plug me with a death bullet. The kid saved my life twice, and Joe Becker remembers that. Once I might forget – but not twice. Anybody here think Will had anything to do with this robbery?"

There was a rumbling of negative answers.

Will opened his eyes and smiled at Mary.

Becker added: "Well then, back up and give these kids room to breathe. Can't you see he's comin' around? Leave him alone with his girl friend!"

30.
Panama, Ten Years Later

The fat man was planted in a chair on the porch of the Panama City Hotel. He was dressed all in white, and a white panama hat shaded his eyes. The skinny fellow at his side was similarly dressed, except that he wore an ill-fitting pith helmet.

The heavy man was reading a letter: "It says that Joey is doin' just fine, and was nine years old on the day Will wrote this letter."

"Joey Becker Seven – I'd like to see him some day," murmured the skinny fellow.

"Well, so would I, so would I – but let's not go back there just yet, eh, Cy? There's so much to do here. Now, according to the treaty, the United States is to start this show on the road with an initial cash payment of ten million – think of that, will you? You know, Cy, it'll take a bit of imagination to smuggle that much money onto a boat to England! Of course, I saw the safe, and it's a cinch. Now, what do you think of this . . ."